WoWStories Volume 1
Sharman Castillo

Contents

Little Sheep

Little Sheep, and Bigger Sheep

Once upon a time, long ago, in a beautiful valley with a lovely lake and rolling hills, there lived a little sheep. There were thousands of other little sheep like her as well. They lived happily with their Shepherd, who took care of them, made sure they were fed and watered daily, and saw that all of their needs were met.

The little sheep were allowed to play and have fun; quite simply, they just enjoyed life. They never had to fear because their Shepherd was mighty and strong and faithful to care for them. The only thing the Shepherd told them to do was to be wary of the big bad wolf on the other side of the fence.

You see, there was a white fence that went all around their land, so they were protected from the wolf. The wolf was much too afraid of the Shepherd to come across the fence and try to get one of the little sheep. So the little sheep obeyed and did as their Shepherd told them because they loved Him with all their hearts, and they knew He loved them. He was good and kind. They could always go to Him when they were feeling down or hurt, because He would listen and heal them. He always went out of His way to make them feel better. He was a good Shepherd.

One day the little sheep were all playing games in different groups. Some played race games, some played hopscotch, and still others played kickball.

In the kickball group, they were having so much fun running after the ball. Yellow Sheep rolled the ball to Blue Sheep, who in turn kicked it so hard it rolled all the way down the hill to the white fence. Little Sheep ran with all her heart, laughing as she went to get it. As she neared the white fence, she slowed down because she saw a Big Red Sheep she had never seen before. The Big Red Sheep was holding the kickball and smiling kindly at Little Sheep, so she went closer and smiled too.

“Are you looking for this ball?” asked the Big Red Sheep.

“Why, yes I am,” said Little Sheep.

“Well, here you go. I have been watching you play with your fellow sheep out there and thought, my, you could be having so much more fun if only you would come over here on this side of the fence.”

"Oh no, Red Sheep, our Shepherd told us never to go over there on that side of the fence, for there is danger."

The Big Red Sheep laughed and said, "Little Sheep, Little Sheep, do I appear to be in any danger? No! Of course I don't. Your Shepherd just does not want you to know that the grass is greener over here on this side of the fence. I tell you, it is. I can show you things you have never seen before and give you things you have never had. You can have your own meadow and your own barn. You could probably even shepherd your own sheep. You do not have to share with anyone. Come, and let me show you."

Little Sheep started to think how much fun it would be to be her own shepherd. Maybe she could have her own little sheep and care for them herself. Just then she heard her Shepherd say, "Little Sheep, where are you? Little Sheep, come here, my love."

But Big Red Sheep said, "Hurry, Little Sheep, hurry, or you will never get your chance to see and have all that I can give to you."

So Little Sheep hurried across the fence right before her Shepherd came within sight of her. The Good Shepherd said, "Little Sheep, what are you doing? Didn't I tell you never to go across the white fence because of the danger? So why have you gone? Do you not care for your safety?" But the Big Red Sheep spoke up and told the Shepherd that he was taking Little Sheep away to see the Real World and that the Shepherd was holding her back.

The Shepherd told Little Sheep, "I love you with all my heart, and I have never lost any of these sheep here that my Father has given to me. I am asking you to stay, but I am not going to force you. You have to want to stay here and trust me because I have your best interest at heart. I would never hurt you or hold you back, but I am asking you not to go, Little Sheep."

Little Sheep shook her head sadly and said, "I am sorry, Shepherd, but I must. The Big Red Sheep is my new friend, and he is going to show me the wonders of the world." On that note, Little Sheep and the Big Red Sheep ran off to see the world. The Shepherd stared sadly after the two and walked back up the hill to the other little sheep, who were confused about what was going on.

The New World

Little Sheep was amazed at all the smells and sights she encountered. Big Red Sheep showed her places where animals went to place bets and were able to win a lot of grain and hay, because you needed grain and hay in order to buy things in the new world. The more grain and hay you had, the richer you were. Little Sheep saw other sheep and animals on corners making what seemed to be deals of some sort, but when she asked the Big Red Sheep, he just laughed and said, "Oh, that's just business."

Big Red Sheep took Little Sheep to many big fancy places and introduced her to a lot of important animals. They all seemed to want Little Sheep's attention. It was a wild and crazy experience for her. She was able to stay up as late as she wanted, and she was even able to eat all the sweets and whatever else she wanted. This was all so new.

Weeks later, after living wildly with a group of new sheep friends she had met when she first got there, a beautiful sheep named Willow asked her, "Little Sheep, do you have a talent or something that you are good at—something that you can do to help pay some of the bills like the rest of us?"

Little Sheep said, "Well, I can sing pretty well. I used to sing for my Shepherd all the time." So Little Sheep started singing, and she sang so well that the other sheep and animals noticed how great she was. She started singing in stables and worked her way up to barns. She became so popular that the animals started paying her to sing for them. Little Sheep became so successful that she made quite a bit of grain and hay. She was able to buy her own meadow and her own barn. Little Sheep was at the top of the world.

What Little Sheep did not know was that while she thought she was making a lot of friends, she was also making a lot of enemies. Willow and the other girl sheep and girl animals were becoming jealous of her because they had lived in their city all their lives and had never reached the fame Little Sheep had reached in such a short time. The other animals started to make plans for how they would take Little Sheep's home, her land, and all of her grain and hay.

One day they told Little Sheep that a very important sheep wanted her to sing at a birthday party and was willing to pay her a lot of hay and grain to do it. Little Sheep was excited and said she would do it. "Where is the party being held, Willow?"

"It is in the barn out by All About Me Lake," said Willow.

"Wow, that is a dark place and no one is ever there," said Little Sheep.

"I know, but it is a big party, so they needed the space. You should be there by eight p.m., so I guess we will see you there."

So Little Sheep went home, took a bath, and made herself smell sweet all over. "If only the other little sheep and my Shepherd could see me now, they would be proud." She got herself ready and started on her way. But when she got there, she saw all of her friends, yet no lights and no party. What they said made her wool cringe.

"Little Sheep, we lied to you to get you here. There is no party. We all want you to know we hate you and do not want you in our town anymore. You have taken all of the best jobs, you have the best home, and more grain and hay than any of us, and you probably even think you are better than us. Well, we are going to teach you a lesson."

Those animals that Little Sheep thought were her friends started to hurt her and call her names. The more she begged for them to stop, the more they hurt her. Then they ran away. Poor Little Sheep could not understand why all of this was happening or why they had done such a terrible thing to her. She had thought they were her friends.

Little Sheep was so hurt and weak that she could barely move, but she managed to make it all the way home. When she finally reached her house, she saw all the lights on, so she crept closer to the window and saw the Big Red Sheep sitting in a chair.

Little Sheep was so relieved that she thought to herself, "I will go in and tell the Big Red Sheep everything that has happened to me, and he will make it all better."

When Little Sheep went inside, she crawled up to where the Big Red Sheep sat and cried, "Oh, Big Red Sheep, they were awful to me and hit me and kicked me and called me names. I don't know why. I have never done anything to them. I was always their friend, and I thought they were mine too. I don't know what is going on!"

The Big Red Sheep looked down at Little Sheep with a frown and said, "Little Sheep, don't you know that it is against the law to enter someone else's house unless they invite you in?"

Little Sheep looked up, confused. "What? This is my house. I live here. What are you talking about?"

Just then Willow walked in wearing Little Sheep's robe and said, "No, Little Sheep, this is my house and everything in it. All of your grain and hay are mine too." She laughed. "So I am going to ask nicely: get out of my house, and if you don't, Big Red and I will throw you out!"

Little Sheep could not believe what was happening to her; her whole world was crashing down around her in mere moments.

She looked at the Big Red Sheep and cried, "Big Red Sheep, do something! You are the one who brought me here. I thought you were my friend. Why won't you help me? Why are you just sitting there?"

The Big Red Sheep laughed and said, "Do you really think that I would be a friend to a mere little sheep like you, especially one who is so pure and sweet? Please. I think that it is time I moved on to more, oh, let us say, exciting pastures."

As he spoke, his nose fell off. He tried to grab it, but as he did, his paw fell off. Little Sheep was in total shock and started to back away. The whole time all of this was taking place, Willow laughed uncontrollably. Finally the Big Red Sheep said, "Forget it. This is more trouble than it is worth." Then he pulled off all of his sheep's clothing, and underneath was a big, ugly wolf.

Little Sheep was terrified and screamed, "Oh my, you were never a sheep at all. You were just a wolf in sheep's clothing!" Little Sheep turned and ran out of the house as fast as she could, which was not very fast because she was so badly hurt. She could hear the wolf and Willow laughing in the background. She ran so far that she lost track of where she was. She came to a ditch and accidentally fell in, slipping all the way down to the bottom. Little Sheep cried and cried; she knew she was lost.

Grace

Little Sheep just did not care anymore and wanted to die, and she had made up her mind to do so. She lay there for hours and gave up on life. Just when she would have taken her last breath, the softest and most gentle touch she had felt since she left home brushed her cheek. "Little Sheep?" Softly and quietly the voice again said, "Little Sheep, wake up, my love. I am here."

Little Sheep opened her eyes and looked up into the eyes of her Shepherd. She was so ashamed that she turned her face away. How could her Shepherd be here when she had turned her back on Him?

"Shepherd, please leave this place. I am bad. I do not deserve for you to be here. You are so good. You do not know all of the bad things I have done since coming to this place. Please go. You have the others, and they need you. Forget about me and let me die."

The Shepherd looked down at Little Sheep with love and kindness on His face. He told her, "Little Sheep, didn't you know that I would leave all nine hundred and ninety-nine of the others in order to come and get you? Do not worry about the others because they are just fine, though they do miss you. If you are willing, I would like to take you home. I do not care what you have done. All I know is that you are sick and very hurt. I can heal you, and I want to heal you, but you must first accept my help. I cannot force it on you. So, if you are willing, may I please take you home? Your brothers and sisters really miss you and love you. So do I."

Little Sheep was so thankful that her Shepherd wanted to take her home. Of course, she knew and felt that she was not worthy, but if she had to die, she wanted it to be with her family and her Shepherd. "Shepherd, I am willing if you will have me. I do not know why you would come all this way for someone like me, but I thank you. The New World was terrible; those animals did not really care about me at all. They only wanted what they could take. The grass was not greener on the other side; it was black. That Big Red Sheep was not my friend. As a matter of fact, he was not even a real sheep; he was just a wolf in sheep's clothing. Please, Shepherd, please take me from this place. I am so sorry!" Little Sheep cried in desperation.

With those words the Shepherd picked Little Sheep up and carried her in His loving arms all the way home. When the

Shepherd got back to the meadow with Little Sheep, He took her to His house and placed her in His own bed. There He and Fluffy Sheep cared for Little Sheep. Little Sheep grew stronger day by day and became healthy again, but the Shepherd would not let her get up; He wanted her to wait until she was completely healed. Little Sheep watched how her Shepherd cared for her, even after all that she had done, and was amazed. Her love for her Shepherd grew stronger and stronger as the days went on.

One day, when the Shepherd and Fluffy Sheep were in the room caring for her, Little Sheep asked the Shepherd, "Shepherd, although I am ever so glad that you found me down in that ditch, how did you? I was lost myself after falling in that ditch. How on earth did you ever find me?"

The Good Shepherd looked at Little Sheep and said, "Little Sheep, a long time ago I once told you that I had never lost any of the sheep my Father had given me, and I had no intention of losing you. As for your being lost, Little Sheep, I knew where you were all along."

Fluffy Sheep walked up to Little Sheep, who was still lying in bed, and kissed her nose. "Little Sheep, do not feel so bad. A long time ago, I went across the fence to the other side too. A lot of bad things happened to me also, and Shepherd was there to rescue me. I asked the Shepherd to forgive me, and I never went back because I realized that this was where I wanted to be."

Fluffy Sheep looked at her Shepherd and said, "Remember, Shepherd?" The Shepherd looked confused, shook His head, and said, "No, Fluffy Sheep, I don't remember that." Fluffy Sheep smiled and winked at Little Sheep. Later, Fluffy Sheep explained to Little Sheep that whenever you asked the Shepherd to forgive you, He totally forgot what it was that you had done after He forgave you. Little Sheep thought about that for a long time and just could not figure it out.

Stand

One day, long ago, in a beautiful valley with a lovely lake, on a rolling hill, Little Sheep stood in the breeze eating her grass. She loved life. She smiled as she breathed in the aroma of fresh flowers in the air. Out of the corner of her eye, a movement caught her attention, and she glanced down the hill to the white fence.

You see, there was a white fence all around their land; it was there to keep the little sheep safe. On the other side of the fence was a group of sheep and animals she once knew long ago. The animals were calling her and begging her to come back over the fence to where they were. They told her that things had changed, that they were sorry, and that they wanted to be her friend again. Little Sheep looked at them; then she looked behind her, where she could see a lovely lake named "Second Chances," where her Shepherd, along with her brothers and sisters, was drinking water.

She felt so much love for them all. She thought to herself, "There is nothing that they can do or give to me that my Shepherd has not already supplied." She then turned and walked away without a second glance, back to join those whom she knew loved and cared for her—her brothers and sisters, and most importantly, her Shepherd.

WOW! Isn't that how Yahuah's love is for us? No matter what we do, if we but humble ourselves and ask for forgiveness, He is not only faithful to forgive us, but He places it in a sea of forgetfulness. And although we may be lost, this great Elohim of ours says that we can be found. Have you asked Him to forgive you? If not, why don't you ask Him now? WoW!

The Invitation

Lisa and Andre

"Oh my gosh, Lisa! Did you hear? It's going to be the greatest ever! I'm going to go and get my invitation right away! What about you?" The happy teen ran down the school hall bursting with excitement.

"Get what? Oh, and like, girl, please get your hand off my arm. You're causing a wrinkle in my blouse," Lisa said. Lisa was one of the most popular girls in school. She was beautiful, well dressed, and came from a wealthy family. All her friends were like her as well; their families were not only very well off but very close too. Tracy, the girl speaking with her now, was no exception.

"Well, I just heard that the most important party of a lifetime is about to take place. The crème de la crème is supposed to be there. It's by invitation only. Can you believe it? I'm going to get my invitation as soon as I see her."

"See who?"

"Vania, you know, the new girl—kind of shy and quiet."

"Oh, then it can't be the crème de la crème, as you say, if she has the invitations. Anyway, who else can we get them from?"

"Lisa, that's just it! No one else seems to know anyone other than Vania who has the invitations. For now, she's the only hope." Suddenly Tracy jumped for joy. "Oh great, there she is! I'm out of here! I must go."

"Oh my gosh! You can't be serious. I know you're not really going over there to beg for an invitation from her?" Lisa rolled her eyes.

"Oh Lisa, why can't you just humble yourself and try to make a new friend? She is not as bad as you think. She really is nice." Tracy shook her head and ran off to talk to Vania, who greeted her with a happy smile.

"Andre, I really don't know why we even bother with Tracy sometimes. She can be so simple-minded and tacky. I mean really, Vania? I don't think she understands just what her position in society is. Next, she'll probably want this Vania to actually hang around with us. Can you imagine?"

Andre smiled at his friend. Lisa had always been a little stuck up about their little group, and he kind of felt the same way, but he also knew he was not going to miss a party this big because of Lisa.

"Well, Lissie, I'm with you, so I plan on going to this party myself, but I can guarantee you I will not lower myself by going over and getting one from this Vania girl either. I'll just wait and see what they look like from others who get one. Then I'll make some fake ones and pass them out to our friends. I'll save you one if you want."

"Oh Andre, you're so smart, but no thank you. I don't need one. I'm sure that once I show up and tell them who I am and they figure out who my family is, they'll usher me right in. As a matter of fact, they should be quite happy to see me." Andre and Lisa finished gathering their books and hurried to their classes before the tardy bell rang.

Vania

"Hey there! I hear you have invitations to the big party that's coming up. I know you don't know me or anything, but my name is Tracy. Umm, I feel kind of embarrassed asking you for an invitation considering the fact that you've been here for a while and I've never taken the time to talk to you before, but here I am now," Tracy said.

Tracy had run up to Vania in order to get an invitation, but now that she was here, she felt pretty guilty because she had never given Vania the time of day, and now here she was asking for one.

Vania gave Tracy a tremendous smile, as though they had been friends all along. "Never be embarrassed to approach me. I've seen you many times before and I already know your name. By the way, I was hoping you would come and ask me for an invitation. I have lots of them, but not many people are asking for any." Vania had an ethereal beauty about her. She was soft-spoken, and as Tracy listened to her now, she felt instantly drawn.

Vania had been at Qodesh High for nearly three months. She had made a lot of friends, but some of the more popular girls were just plain cruel to her, and she could not understand why they had not even given her a chance. Still, she chose not to hold it against them. Vania understood how it was to be a teen. Little did they know, had they dared to come up to her, she would have embraced their friendship immediately.

"Well, may I have one for myself and two more for my friends?" Tracy asked, barely able to control her joy.

"I'm sorry, Tracy, I can only give you one, because anyone else who wants one has to ask me personally. I hope you understand."

"Oh, of course. I'm just happy to have mine. Um, Vania, you know I don't have a dress to wear to this party, and I thought that maybe we could go shopping at the mall together. What do you think?" Tracy felt kind of shy suddenly. However, Tracy did not realize she had just made Vania incredibly happy.

The girls agreed to meet on the following day, which was Thursday. The big event was on Saturday night after the Shabbat, so they did not have much time. Tracy ran to her next class holding her invitation tightly. Vania went to her next class hoping more people would ask for an invitation.

Friday

"Hey Lisa! Have you gotten your invitation yet?"

When Lisa shook her head no, Tracy was appalled. "The party is tomorrow, and Vania said that only those who actually came up to her personally would receive an invitation. What is wrong with you? Don't you even want to go to this party?" Tracy could not understand Lisa's pride on this matter. Vania was such a sweet person, and as far as she could tell, Lisa was being unreasonable by not wanting to ask for her own invitation.

"Like I told Andre, I really am looking forward to going to the party, Tracy! Which is lucky for them that I want to go at all. I just don't feel like I must bow down and ask Vania for anything. I can just show up, you know. The people in this town know who I am and who my family is. Just because you felt like it was important to lower yourself like a commoner doesn't mean you need to force me. In addition to that, if it becomes necessary for me to have an invitation, then Andre has made some of his own and he'll give me one." Lisa was super irritated at this point, so she got up and left the table where they were having lunch in the cafeteria to go eat with some other girls at another table.

The Party

The big night had finally arrived, and the whole town buzzed with excitement. In the middle of Town Square, the huge Banqueting Hall had been transformed into something out of a fairytale. Lights blazed from all the windows, and the most beautiful music ever heard drifted outside. People's voices were raised in conversation and laughter. The line was long, leading up the stairs to the entrance.

A butler, richly dressed in a white uniform with gold braid running down his arms and chest, checked each invitation as the guests came up the stairs.

Lisa, Tracy, Andre, and a group of their friends stood at the end of the line. Lisa was upset because they had arrived so late to the party and now were in the back. Fortunately, they did not have to wait too long, because the line was moving quickly.

Andre once again tried to offer Lisa a fake invitation, but she declined, stating that she had it on good authority that all she had to do was state her name.

"Invitations, please?" the butler at the top of the stairs asked the last group to enter.

"Yes, well, my name is Lisa, and I'm from the Yahudi family. I'm sure you have heard of us."

"Yahudi. Yes, I do seem to recall that name. It's a rather large tribe. How are you this evening, young lady?"

"Fine, I guess," Lisa replied. She was a little annoyed that he had not instructed the footmen to open the doors for her yet. "Well?"

"Well, in order to enter this party, you have to have an invitation. You do have an invitation, don't you?" the butler asked Lisa again.

Lisa stood back in stunned silence, realizing for the first time that this man was actually not going to let her into the party without an invitation.

"Sir! I have an invitation," Tracy spoke up.

The butler smiled, took the invitation she offered, and held it up under a fluorescent light to examine it. Then he looked at Tracy and smiled again; he looked up to where the footmen stood and nodded his head. The two footmen who stood on either side of the big double doors opened them. The light from within was blinding, and the music and gaiety overwhelming. Tracy entered, and then the doors closed again.

"Invitations, please," the butler said to Andre, who handed him his invitation.

The butler smiled as he put Andre's invitation up to the light, but then he frowned. "Sir, this invitation is not authentic. I'm sorry, but if this is the invitation you are presenting, it will not get you in here. You too should have gotten an invitation from Vania; they were free and given freely as well."

"What! Why do you think this is fake? This is a real invitation. I got it from Vania myself," Andre said. He was super embarrassed but also desperate, because he just had to go into that party. He could not bear to miss it.

"I'm sorry, sir, but this is a fake invitation. I know it is because, you see, when you place this invitation up to the light, in the right-hand corner there appears, in little lettering, 'This is my friend,' with the initial V. Sir, if this is the invitation you and your friends are going to present, then I'm sorry. You must have the real thing in order to enter." The butler walked back to his position.

The unhappy group of teenagers stood where they were and could not believe that they were not going into what seemed like the most amazing party ever. Lisa's eyes began to water. Why had she not lowered her pride and just asked Vania for the invitation? She would now be inside having so much fun with everyone else. She felt excluded, and she knew she had brought it on herself.

While Lisa and the group she had come with were still standing at the top of the stairs, a beautiful white Rolls-Royce drove up. The chauffeur stopped the car and got out. He went around to the other side and opened the rear passenger door. Out stepped the most handsome and distinguished man Lisa had ever seen. The man turned and reached his hand back down to the open car door, and out stepped Vania, dressed in a beautiful white gown. She took hold of the older man's hand. Vania looked lovely, and excitement shone all over her face. When they got to the top of the stairs, the butler and both footmen bowed their heads as they opened the doors to let them in.

Lisa stared at the butler and said, "Hey! Why did you just let her in without an invitation?"

"Madam, I let them in because this party was thrown in her honor by her Father. I know that everyone was told of this upcoming party. I even know that she passed the invitations out personally herself. All anyone had to do was ask, and she was eager for all to attend. I suppose some were not willing to seek her out. Why, I do not know, but it is their loss. Now, if you will excuse me, the footmen and I were invited as well."

The butler then reached into his coat pocket and produced an invitation. "Good night." The butler and the footmen then turned and left Lisa, Andre, the rest of their group, as well as many others who had just shown up, standing at the top of the stairs while they went inside to join the others for the greatest party ever held.

WOW! Isn't that what Yahuah has done in our case? He has sent His Son, our Mashiach Yahshua, to pass out invitations to all who will repent and ask Him into their hearts. For there is no other way to the Father but by His Son. So on that day when we all stand before a righteous and Qodesh Elohim, do you have your invitation—the Ruach HaQodesh? WOW!

The Bigger Picture

Sonya

The sun was bright outside Sonya Taylor's house; she could see it gleaming through her curtains. She got out of bed and made her way down the hallway to the bathroom. She peered into the mirror and winced. Her eyes were puffy and bloodshot red. Oh heck, this was going to be another argument for her mother to start, and she just did not want to deal with it.

After washing her face and finishing up in the bathroom, she made her way back to her bedroom to get dressed for the day. She put on a pair of hip-hugger jeans and a shirt high enough to show her belly ring; then she pulled her long brunette hair back into a ponytail.

Sonya was a natural beauty, so she did not wear much makeup at all. As soon as she was finished putting on her shoes, she grabbed her backpack and ran down the hall, down the stairs, and out of the house.

Sonya wanted to avoid her mother at all costs. She loved her, and Mom could be cool at times, but they lived on different planets. Her mother was always telling her how God had wonderful plans for her and that if she would only give God a try, she would see. Well, Sonya was having too much fun to consider that right now. She was young, pretty, and in a great position at her job.

Sonya was twenty-one and had graduated from college five months earlier. She had earned her bachelor's degree in network administration and landed a job with the top fashion magazine in the state of New York as the overseer of their database. So not only was she important behind the scenes, but she was also important out front because she got to talk to reporters, models, lawyers, and all of the bigwigs. Her office was laid back and youthful, so the atmosphere was more than casual. She did not know how God had made plans for her without asking her opinion, but she was not ready for anything else right now.

"Sonya, there's a meeting in an hour, and it doesn't sound good," Shelby, one of her assistants, said.

"What do you mean?"

"Rumor has it that the company wants to downsize," Shelby whispered.

"Well, what has that got to do with us? I practically run this place," Sonya told her.

"No, Sonya, this is serious!"

"Don't worry about it." Sonya shook her head.

Later, in the meeting, Mr. Price, one of the CEOs, looked very uncomfortable as he spoke. "I'm sorry, but that means half of you are going to have to be let go, and the half we've chosen are here in this room now. That means all of you. I'm sorry."

"Kevin, I don't get it. How can you lay me off when my job is supposed to be secure? That is why I chose this company over the others who wanted to hire me. I mean, I'm the one who runs your database." Sonya was outraged.

"I know, Sonya, and I understand your anger. It is just that the board has decided to go with the supercomputer that virtually runs itself."

"Even a supercomputer needs someone to run it!" Sonya shouted.

At the sound of Sonya's tone, Mr. Price took on another attitude. "That may be so, my dear, but you won't be running it." Mr. Price and the other managers then left the room. The laid-off employees were left to discuss their situation, gather their things, and leave.

Mama Way

"Sonya!" Mrs. Taylor knocked louder on the door. Finally she opened it, walked over to her daughter's bed, and pulled back the covers. "Get up! I mean it. Get up right now and come downstairs!"

"Oh Mom! Please!" Sonya took the sheets and pulled them back over her head.

"No! I mean it right now. Don't make me come back up here, because if I do, I'll drag you downstairs." With that, Mrs. Taylor went back downstairs.

Ten minutes later, Sonya sat down across from her younger sister.

"What a loser. Did you bother to brush your teeth?" Tammy wrinkled her nose.

"See, Mom, that's why I wanted to stay in my room," Sonya whined.

"That's enough, Tammy! But I'm not going to baby you either. It's been two months already, and you still don't have a job, and you're still moaning about the past, and I'm sick of it. Get over it and get a job—any job." Mrs. Taylor was actually a good-looking woman at thirty-nine and could easily have passed for Sonya's sister, but today she did not care who she appeared to be. She was a mother first, and she was sick of her daughter's pity party affecting everyone in the house.

"I've tried to get a job. All of the places that once wanted to hire me already have somebody, and the other places I at least tried to apply to have all closed their doors. I don't know what to do. I have bills. I'm almost out of money," Sonya said.

"How can you almost be out of money? You don't pay rent or utilities. Mom and Dad do," Tammy questioned.

"I have a Beemer and student loans, thank you!" Sonya couldn't stand her sister.

"Well, that's your problem if you didn't save or spend your money wisely. But I do know this: you might be looking too high. You need to come down to earth for a little while, honey. Get the job you can, and God will open a door."

"Mom! Stop it! I have too much education and too many abilities to go and flip burgers."

"Well, your education isn't doing too much in your favor, so you better get what you can. I'm not paying anything, Sonya, and guess what? I can afford it, but you're too prideful, so I'm going to let you do this on your own. So that car—you know, your Beemer—it's going to have to go, and you'll have to get a less expensive one. And flipping burgers? You may just have to do that for a while." Mrs. Taylor walked over and kissed the top of her daughter's bent head. "Oh, and one last thing: your father said to tell you we are all going to Bible study tonight, and so are you."

"I don't think so," Sonya said.

"Oh yes you are! Daddy said he wasn't asking you; he was telling you."

This was the only thing Sonya liked at church—the praise and worship music. She could do that all day, but when the pastor got up, she grimaced.

Sonya sat there and did not pay attention the whole night until, at the end of the service, something the pastor said caught her attention.

"Sometimes when God is calling an individual and His plans in your life are beginning to come alive, God will begin to manipulate your surroundings. You'll lose your job, your car, your friends, and anything else that's distracting. Can I get a witness? You can do whatever you want to try and run, but Jesus will apprehend you in the end. Why run from the inevitable? Don't you feel that longing in your heart? Don't you think something is missing? You've tried everything else—why not try Jesus? I guarantee you won't be disappointed. And if you're not happy, go back." The pastor wiped his brow with a cloth. "Now if this message is for you and you think somehow God might be calling you, then don't sit there. Come down here now and cry out to Jesus. Let Him be your sure tower of refuge. Let Him change your life. Let Him heal you. Let Him deliver you."

The music began to play, and Sonya watched as people young and old got out of their seats to go forward. She did not want to go just to make her mother happy, but there was a pulling on her heart. She wanted to feel what all of these other people were feeling, so she made her decision and stepped out of her seat. On the way, she had to indicate to her father and mother that they needed to move so she could pass. Her mother had her eyes closed, but her father was able to pull her out of the way. As Sonya passed and began to make her way forward, she could hear her mother begin to cry and thank Jesus. How embarrassing.

This was the most humiliating walk ever; everyone knew she was a heathen, according to their vernacular. With every step, her heartbeat sounded louder and louder in her ears, but she was determined. She wanted what these people had—joy. If God could make her life right, as her mother and everyone else said, then she would give Him a try.

The pastor said a prayer and had everyone at the altar, and even those still in the congregation, repeat it. Sonya meant every word, so she began to cry, and it felt so good. People came up to the altar to welcome them into the family of Christ.

"Saints, you now belong to Jesus. I want you to promise that you'll read your Bible every day and attach yourself to a home church. It may not be here and it may be, but ask God to lead you, and He will. Now God bless you all." The pastor turned and left the pulpit.

As soon as Sonya turned around, her mother was there to gather her into her arms.

Sonya did exactly as the pastor had told her. She began to read her Bible every day, and her relationship with God grew. She joined the church her mother attended, and even her relationship with her sister changed. She had prayed and asked God to take full control of her life and told Him she was more than willing to submit to Him in everything.

Still, every door remained closed to her where jobs were concerned. She finally humbled herself and went to the local café and applied. She was hired on the spot. Her duties were waiting tables and cashiering. What a change—to go from making close to five thousand dollars a month and driving a Beemer to making one thousand dollars a month and driving a Honda. Although there is nothing wrong with a Honda, it was just a big change.

She worked for Lou's Café for eight whole months when Lou called all of the employees into his office. "Okay, gang, I've called you all into my office today because I have some important news for you. It seems that business is going to stay slow for a while, and since it is, I'm going to have to let you all go except for the cook and two waitresses. I'm sorry, guys, but

I just can't afford to pay everyone. I really hope you understand. I am, of course, keeping my wife on as head waitress and cashier. I kept Thelma as a waitress as well just because she's been here the longest. I hope you all can understand. You can finish out the rest of the week, and then I'm going to have to let you go."

Nobody said a thing. There was nothing to say. Everyone knew that if Lou could have avoided laying them off, he would have. It was not the first time some of them had been laid off by Lou.

Sonya, on the other hand, was devastated, although she did not let it show. How could God let this happen? He knew her situation. She had, after all, taken this job hoping He would open some other door for her, but instead He seemed to kick her out of this one too. What was going on?

Later that night, as she lay in bed crying, she heard a soft tap on the door.

"Come in," she sniffed.

Mrs. Taylor came and lay on the bed next to Sonya. She took her daughter in her arms and began to stroke her head.

"Honey, it's not as bad as you think," her mother said, trying to comfort her.

"It is. I don't get it, Mom. I told God to take control of my life and I trusted Him. I mean, I humbled myself like the Bible says and took a job waiting on tables and actually liked it." Sonya cried. "I don't know what God wants from me, Mom. I have a bachelor's degree in network administration, but I liked taking orders and serving people. I loved it, and now it too is gone. Is God mad at me?"

"No, honey, God is not mad or angry with you. Sometimes God allows things to happen, but He has a bigger plan for us all. Just trust Him. Don't let circumstances dictate whether you'll serve God or not." Her mother hugged and kissed her again. "I was meaning to tell you, honey: at church they are hiring for housekeeping."

"Oh Mom, come on now," Sonya moaned.

"I know, but at least it's a foot in the door."

"Fine. What time do I need to apply?" Sonya asked with a surrendered smile.

"Eight a.m.," Mrs. Taylor said.

God's Way

Sonya began working at New Believers Christian Center as their custodian. At first it was embarrassing to go in and clean a bathroom when people she knew would come in to use the restroom, but she soon got used to it and it did not bother her any longer. Sonya would move through the offices singing to the music coming out of her iPod. The people loved her because she was efficient and quiet.

About five months into her job, Sonya was outside the main business office getting ready to empty the trash when her iPod stopped working. She looked at it, trying to get it to work, but then she realized it only needed to be charged. She took it off and put it into her jacket pocket. Then she went quietly into the office because she knew there were still people working inside.

"Oh my gosh, Sandy, you've wiped out the entire database! This can't be happening. What are we going to do?" Albert and the rest of the staff hovered over Sandy's desk trying to figure out what to do.

"Okay, let's try this again. Tell me exactly what you did," Tom, the Business Administrator, asked.

"I just don't remember. We are never going to figure this out. Pastor is going to kill me for this," Sandy said, beside herself.

"No, Pastor is going to kill us all, because this is going to cost a fortune to replace. He may even replace us," Albert moaned.

"Excuse me," Sonya said. When she did not get a response, she said a little louder, "Excuse me!"

The staff turned around and acknowledged her with a nod. Tom even moved out of the way so she could reach the trash. She did grab the trash and empty it, but then she mustered up the courage to say, "Not to be intrusive or anything, but I think I might be able to help."

"Thanks, honey, but if Tom can't figure it out, then nobody can."

"Well, I really think I can help. I know something about computers, and maybe if you told me, I could look and see whether there is something I could do." Sonya could see them all hesitate, so she added, "What have you got to lose? None of you can figure it out. If I solve it, it'll save you thousands, and if I don't, you're no worse off."

"That's true, and since I'm the one responsible, I give you my permission to help." Sandy got up from her desk and offered Sonya her seat. "Okay, I have two databases that I keep on my desktop—one of the church members and one of their tithing records. I thought I was deleting backup copies of the databases when, in actuality, I deleted the originals. We cannot find them. They are called *Members Info* and *Tithing Records.*"

"Okay, give me about fifteen minutes." Sonya sat down and rebooted the computer to start in D.O.S. She then began a search of records still on the hard drive. After finding what she needed and reactivating the records so they would start in Windows, she got up. "There you go!" she said with a smile.

"Amazing! Absolutely amazing! How did you do that?" Tom asked with admiration.

"I went to school and studied it," Sonya said, and began to walk away. "Well, thank you!" they all called as she finished what she was doing and then left the room.

About a week later, when Sonya was in the bathroom cleaning the commodes, the bathroom door was flung open and her name was called.

"Sonya! Sonya! Oh please be here! There you are! Come quick! Albert opened his email today and attached to it was a virus. Do you know what to do?" Sandy asked in desperation.

"It depends on how much damage has been done." When she got there, she realized that a lot of damage had been done. So she quarantined the virus and saved all of the important work to rewritable disks. Sonya had to wipe the hard drive clean and reinstall Windows and every other program that had been there in the first place. It took her five hours, and she was exhausted. Everybody was so happy that another disaster had been avoided. Then Sonya left to finish the rest of her job cleaning the church.

She did not make it home until nine o'clock that night. She was so tired it was pathetic. She still did her Bible study and prayed. She was relieved when she finally went to sleep, and she rested deeply.

Early the next morning, Sonya got up and prepared herself for work. She could smell bacon downstairs. She was in a cheery mood. She had slept so well it was unbelievable. She went downstairs, and her mother smiled as she sat at the table.

"You look happy," Mrs. Taylor commented.

"I am, Mom. You know, yesterday I felt useful. I was able to help, and it made me feel good."

"Good for you." Mrs. Taylor walked over and put a piece of paper in front of her. "Last night when you came in, I was asleep, so I was unable to give you this message. It seems the pastor wants a meeting with you this morning at nine, so you'll have to hurry."

"Oh Mom! You should have woken me up. I only have half an hour!" Sonya drank the rest of her orange juice and ran out of the house.

"Sonya, I am so happy you made it." Pastor stood to shake her hand as she walked into the room.

"Thank you, Pastor, but I only found out this morning. My mother was asleep when I got home last night."

“That’s fine. Have a seat.” Pastor sat down and smiled. “I called you in here today because I’ve heard such wonderful things about you. Twice, I hear, you’ve saved the church thousands of dollars. Believe me, the Bible says to give credit where credit is due. My staff has credited you with blessing the church, and you never asked for anything or drew attention to your abilities, so I want to bless you by offering you a position of leadership. I want you to come on staff as Church Administrator.”

“Pastor, I am honored! Oh my gosh—wow!” Sonya was beside herself. “Pastor, you don’t know how badly I want this, but I can’t.”

“Why on earth not?” the pastor asked.

“Because I couldn’t take Tom’s job from him, sir,” Sonya said.

The pastor began to laugh and sat back down. “Oh honey, didn’t you know that God doesn’t raise one without raising another to take his or her place?”

“What do you mean?” Sonya asked.

"I have promoted Tom to Associate Pastor. He's a godly man, and I think he's wasting what God has given him; he needs to be spreading the gospel to people directly. It was Tom who recommended you. He said you possessed the talent and abilities he himself did not."

"Oh, praise God! Yes sir, I'll take it!" Sonya ran around the desk and hugged her pastor.

Sonya began working as the Church Administrator, and it went perfectly. She knew that this was what God had called her to do. She redid every program the church had been using and created more user-friendly databases. She even created a database where monthly graphs on attendance and giving could be pulled up quickly.

Sonya was extremely happy, and so were the pastor and the rest of the staff. Her relationship with the Lord continued to grow. She and the other members of the staff were required to take different courses that the pastor or one of his associates would offer for spiritual growth.

This continued for a year, and it was the happiest year of Sonya's entire life. One day the pastor called Sonya into his office and told her that one of the other pastors in the city, who had a big congregation, was impressed with the smooth running of their church and wanted to know how it was kept so organized. Of course, he had told him about Sonya.

Hearing about Sonya's abilities led him to ask whether it would be possible to have Sonya come over and set up a database for his church like the one they had at New Believers Christian Center. Of course, Pastor allowed her to go. He even let her go to two other churches in the city that had heard about her abilities. On her fourth trip out, she stayed a week training a particular staff member at a church.

When she came back on Monday morning, she was shocked to find a new woman sitting at her desk.

"Good morning," the woman looked up.

"Good morning, and please don't take this rudely; I don't even know how to say this, but you're sitting at my desk."

"Oh! I am sorry. Pastor told me you'd be in this morning to train me," the woman said, getting up.

Pastor walked into the room, having heard Sonya's voice. "Oh, I didn't expect you in so early, Sonya. I didn't get a chance to talk to you at service yesterday. I'm sorry. This here is Agnes Carmichael; she's going to be taking your place, so I need you to train her. She already has a bachelor's degree in computer science, but I need her to know what we do here."

"Oh, okay. Where do I put my stuff?" Sonya said in embarrassment.

"Well, I don't think Agnes would mind if you put your stuff behind her desk until you finish training her. Would you, Agnes?"

"Oh no, not at all!" Agnes opened a drawer for her. "I put all of your personal effects in a box. Pastor put them in that big room at the end of the hall."

"Oh, okay," Sonya said. Inside, her heart hit the floor. Not again. Not again. She was losing her job again, and this time God had her training her replacement. It took all the strength she had to finish out the rest of the day.

The next week seemed a blur. All she could think of was what she had done to deserve this. She had thought for sure that this was where God had called her to be. At the end of the week, on Friday, when she was on her way down the hall to get her things out of the room where Agnes said she had placed them, Pastor stopped her and called her into his office.

Sonya went into his office to see what it was that he wanted. Her heart hurt so badly that she did not know what to do. Since she was in his office, she was going to ask for a referral to maybe one of the other churches. She hoped he would give it to her.

"My dear Sonya, you've been so busy lately. I talked to Agnes, and she said you trained her well. I knew you would." He smiled.

"Thank you, Pastor," Sonya said, barely able to suppress her tears.

"My dear, whatever is the matter?" Pastor asked, concerned.

"Nothing, sir."

"No, I want to know now, Sonya. What is it?"

"Well, Pastor, I'm really embarrassed, considering today is my last day." At her words, the pastor jumped up and his eyes widened. "I don't know what to say. This week has been a blur.

I just can't believe I'm losing my job again for the third time. I had thought for sure that this was where God had called me to be. I don't know." Sonya then began to cry.

The pastor's wide-eyed look disappeared as Sonya continued talking. Realization finally settled in, and he understood. He walked around his desk and hugged the sobbing girl. Then he handed her some tissues and sat back down. "My dear, please stop crying." He began to chuckle.

Sonya stopped crying and looked at Pastor as if he were crazy.

"I'm not laughing at you. I'm laughing at me. I was so happy for you that I forgot to tell you entirely." Pastor stood and motioned for her to sit down. As soon as she did, he sat too. "My dear Sonya, you haven't lost your job. Haven't you gone down the hall to where we put your stuff?"

"No, I was on my way there when you called." Sonya was still upset that he had laughed at her. It was not funny.

"Well, dear, that's your new office!" he said.

"No!" Sonya jumped up.

"Yes! My dear, we are not kicking you out. God is promoting you. I told you God doesn't promote one without promoting another to take your place. Agnes has been promoted from Administrative Assistant to your old position. You have been promoted to Minister. You have diligently been a seeker of the Lord. You are humble and wise. God has called you to go throughout the world and establish smooth-running administrations for His body. That means you are going to go throughout the United States and help other churches set up their systems with the different software you have developed here at our church and others you've visited. Pastors have been so impressed with what you've done that they are begging for you to come to their churches. All expenses paid. They want you to train their staff and everything. They even want you to go to different countries with them to help plant new churches. Sonya, they are talking about paying you twenty and thirty thousand dollars apiece for your time!" Pastor smiled.

"Me?" Sonya asked in shock.

"Yes, you, Sonya. God hasn't demoted you; He's promoted you. Now step into your prophetic future with confidence." Sonya could not believe what the pastor had just told her.

Later, after Pastor had assured her that what he had just said was true, Sonya began to praise God. She left his office and headed down the hall. She opened the door to the office and stood in amazement. There was all of her stuff, organized and beautiful. This office was just a little smaller than Pastor's. On her desk was a nameplate that read, 'Minister Sonya Taylor.'

Her blessing had been there all the time. All she had to do was open the door.

WoW! Isn't that wonderful? God allowed Sonya to go from a great job to a job as a waitress. Why? So she could learn to serve. Then He allowed her to be a housekeeper. Why? So she could learn humility. Then He gave her a desk out front and allowed her to become comfortable, and then He put someone else in her place. Why? So she could learn to move. You see, no matter what, God has a bigger picture for us all. His plans supersede anything we could have hoped for or imagined. So wait on God. He will do what He said He would do, He will stand by His Word, and He will come through! WoW!

The Sentence

"Will the defendant please stand," the judge addressed the defendant and his attorney. "You have been found guilty of the assault and killing of Karen Fisher. We will now hear the punishment that the jury deemed sufficient."

There was absolute silence in the courtroom as the foreman of the jury stood to hand a piece of paper to the bailiff. The bailiff then took the paper to the judge, who read its contents. The judge then nodded to the foreman, who turned and faced the defendant's table.

"We the jury, having found you, David Carrington, guilty of the assault and killing of Karen Fisher, sentence you to die by lethal injection." The foreman then nodded to the judge, who nodded back.

"Mr. Carrington, the jury has sentenced you to death by lethal injection. Because of the 'Shepard Case' back in 2020, the appellate court has been abolished. So this sentence will take place in six months from this day, on April 21, 2026, the day after what was formerly known as Easter Sunday." The judge paused for a long moment to let his words sink in, and then he continued. "Do you have anything you'd like to say to the family of the deceased or the court?"

The defendant stared hard at the judge and then turned around to stare at the family of the deceased girl. He smiled—or rather snarled out a grin—and said, "If I had it to do over again, I would still do it. Your girl was like a wildcat." He threw back his head and laughed.

At that point, there was utter chaos in the courtroom. Both the father and brother of Karen Fisher were so upset that they lunged at David Carrington, and he had to be removed from the courtroom.

The Cell

David paced his cell like a caged animal. He was sick of this place. He had been there a whole month and still had five months before they killed him. The only people he ever saw were the guards and that stupid guy who came to taunt him because he was the one who would administer the lethal dose that would kill him.

He never left the cell, period. The only way he would ever be able to leave it was if he requested to attend church on Sundays or Wednesdays, or he could go to assembly with some men claiming to be Israelites on Saturdays, and he had refused to do either. He sure as heck didn't believe in a white Jesus who had never done anything for Black people in the first place, and he didn't know who in the world this black Yahusha was supposed to be either. He had given up on God a long time ago, and those men were saying that they didn't even use that word—they called Him Elohim.

He remembered being a young boy of nine when his mother had died. She had been a Christian. The pastor had told him not to cry but to rejoice because she was with the Lord. The pastor had also said that anyone who asked Jesus into his or her heart and confessed their sins would be saved. Now he heard that Christianity was a cult of confused people. He was super confused.

He remembered one night after his mother had passed that he had dreamed he was walking with Jesus and a group of children in the front yard of his house. He had been so happy. In the dream, David had looked up into the face of Jesus and asked, "Jesus, will you forgive me of my sins?"

The Jesus in his dream had looked down at him and said, "No." Then he walked on with the little white children, holding their hands and smiling.

A simple dream had destroyed him forever, and he had figured that if he was going to go to hell one day anyway, he might as well live like hell. When he had met Karen Fisher at a nightclub, his intention was not to kill her. He had actually thought she was cute. He had bought drinks for himself and for her all night long, and he thought that she liked him.

He found out differently near the end of the night when he overheard her talking on her cell phone. "Hey Tina, I'm about out of here. I just have to find a way to dump this idiot who's been buying me drinks all night." She had laughed and then continued, "Please, I was out of money and Sean doesn't get off till three, so I had to kill time. Okay, you too. Love ya, bye."

Dave had become angry, realizing that she had used him, and he wanted to make her hurt like he was hurting. So he had waited outside, and it had all gone wrong. She died, and there was nothing he could do to bring her back. He did not even remember it happening, but oh well, it did. Dave looked through the bars and stared straight ahead.

The next afternoon, as David was lying on his bed, the guard Steve Martin came to taunt him.

"So, you counting the days?" Steve cackled.

"Counting the days for what?" David answered.

"You know, till I pull the plug and send you to hell where you belong."

"No, I'm not counting them, but when I get there, I'll save you a seat." David had propped himself up onto one arm.

"You sorry piece of trash? I ain't going to hell with you criminals." The guard grabbed the bars.

"I don't see how you figure that. There are only two places you can go—heaven or hell—and I know you're not going to heaven." David laughed.

"You shut your mouth if you know what's good for you! Everybody goes to heaven except people like you!"

"Hey, you two! Calm down. Sorry to get involved, but I just can't stand here and listen to you both believe a lie." A tall, light-skinned Black man came and stood near Steve.

"Oh, hey, preacher of what-I-don't-know-you're-preaching," Steve said.

"What seems to be the problem?" Rick, who was in charge of the prison ministry program, asked.

"Well, I was telling this here sinner that he is going to hell and that I am not. I'm a good person, and good people don't go to hell," Steve said for all to hear.

"Well, Steve, my man, you're wrong. Good people go to hell also. No one is exempt except those who believe in HaMashiach."

"That's what's wrong with you religious zealots. You're always trying to force your particular religion on people, but all are the same. They all point to God," Steve said.

"That's where you're wrong, my friend. The Bible says that there is no other name under heaven by which we might be saved except the name Yahusha HaMashiach, whom many call

Jesus Christ. However, since the Word says that there is power in His name, I use His Hebrew name. Buddha and Muhammad didn't die for you. Gandhi didn't die for you. But Yahusha did. The Bible says that there is no other door unto the Father that man can go through unless they come by His Son. So you see, there is no other way. Whether you wish to believe it or not, Yahusha is the only way." Rick explained with love and patience, but he was also firm, with authority in his voice.

"Whatever, preacher man. You believe what you believe, and I'll believe what I want to believe." Steve started to walk away.

"Wait a moment, man. I know this may seem strange to you, but I am more than willing to stay and talk and pray with you. It would give me great pleasure to explain to you what I know concerning Yahusha." Rick said with a smile.

"It's all right." Steve sneered at David, then nodded to Moreh Rick and walked away.

Rick and David watched as Steve walked away shaking his head. Rick turned around again to face David and said, "You know, he was also wrong when he said that you were destined to go to hell. You don't have to go, you know. You can accept the gift that Abba Yahuah gave you and believe on His Son.

Yahusha was sent to redeem a lost people to their heritage, to wake them up to who they truly are. Do you know who you are?"

David shook his head.

"Well, you are an Israelite—more than likely from the tribe of Judah. We are the actual people that the Bible speaks about. We were all brought over here on slave ships because of what our ancestors did, totally separated from Yah. We were all lost. It's amazing. You have to read Deuteronomy 28, my man. It is wonderful to give your heart and life to Yahusha so that He can forgive all your sins. But man, there is even more. You can have an actual relationship with the Father and the Son. On that day when you take your last breath, you'll wake up in glory."

"I'm sorry, preacher, but I don't believe any of that junk. Jesus—or as you call Him, Yahusha—rejected me long ago when I was a child, and He doesn't want me now, and I don't want Him." David turned in his cell and walked back to his bunk and sat down.

Rick crouched in front of David's cell and began to speak. "You know, man, I know that you've only got five months left to live. I know you're trying to be tough and big and bad, but why? No one can really see you here, and no one here cares. You're locked up. You never leave your cell, and you never have any visitors except me or others in ministry with me."

"That's not true. Steve is faithful to torment me every single day."

"Yeah, that's true, but you know what I mean. Why don't you just come, if only for the sake of getting out of your cell once or twice a week? What can it hurt? If you don't like it, then don't come back."

"I don't know. I'm really just not interested. I'm okay with going to hell. I have been for as long as I can remember." David turned away.

"Okay, that's a start. We have a meeting tomorrow night at six. If you're there, you are, and if not, you're not." Rick stood up.

"Fine." David lay down on his bunk and closed his eyes. So the Moreh walked away humming a song, while David thought to himself about all that he had heard. Him, an Israelite? He figured it would be good just to get out and be around other people. He would not participate at all, but he would go so he didn't feel so lonely.

Fellowship

David did not attend Bible study the next night because Steve the guard made it hard for him to go, but he did start the following Saturday on what they called a Shabbat. David never participated in any of the discussions, but he did listen. He was given his own Bible to read, but he seldom picked it up.

This went on for four months. He listened to hardened criminals talk about the love of the Most High, and he could see the change in people who had joined the group after him. He also remembered coming into assembly or Bible study and knowing that Paul, or Morris, or Gene would not be there because they had died that day or night. He had never been afraid to die before, but now he was becoming afraid. What if what all these people were saying was true? What if hell was real and he really was going to wake up in an eternal nightmare? What if? What if?

He could feel something in his chest that made him feel a longing sensation—but longing for what? He knew he could not accept Jesus because Jesus had told him in that dream when he was a kid that He would never forgive him. But he was confused, because the Jesus he grew up hearing about apparently was not the Yahusha these men were talking about. This man seemed to look like him and the people he grew up with. Same book, but different people entirely.

He kicked the chair in front of him without thinking.

"Is there a problem, David?" Moreh Rick asked him.

"Yeah, I have a problem, but it can't be fixed." David looked uncomfortable.

"We don't know if we can fix the problem or not, David, unless you tell us."

"No one can." David looked angry.

"Look, tell me," Rick said.

David looked as though he would refuse, but then he began to speak. "Okay, say you're a little kid and you have a dream. In the dream you're walking with Jesus. You look up with childlike innocence and say, 'Jesus, will you forgive me of my sins?' Then Jesus looks down at you and says no. How would you feel, knowing that Jesus would never forgive you of your sins and that you're going to hell no matter what?"

Finally he had said it, and Moreh Rick understood. David could not give his life to Yahusha because the stronghold in his life was deceit. He had believed what a false messiah had told him in a dream all those years, and now he was bound by fear, thinking Yahuah and Yahusha would reject him. Rick finally knew that David was ripe for the picking; he just needed to know the truth.

"David, that is a lie from hell—from the enemy of the Father to keep you in chains. Yahuah would never come to you in a dream and tell you He would not forgive your sins. That is not His way, especially not to a child of Yashar'el. That is a deceptive maneuver the enemy employs. You're not the first, and you won't be the last, to fall for that lie. I had a similar thing happen to me as a child."

"When I was young, I had a compulsive disorder. I thought that if I kept repeating, 'I love you, Yah. I love Yahusha. I love your Ruach, and I hate haSatan in the name of Yahusha,' then I would be protected. It got so bad that I found myself repeating the phrase over and over, as if I had not said it right the first ten times. One night, while I was in bed, I was repeating it again and again when I accidentally said, 'I love Yah, I love Yahusha,' but I did not say that I loved the Ruach in the name of Yahusha."

"I misspoke, and it scared me so badly that I couldn't move. I knew for sure that I had just blasphemed the Ruach and that I was going to go to hell. I thought that for years. I became involved in drugs, drinking, and any other thing you could think of until one day the Most High apprehended me. I mean, man, I knew it was a hopeless case for me, but Yahusha came into my life. I surrendered myself to Him, hoping that maybe He could help. I knew He heard my prayer when I gave my heart to Him, but it was still hard for me to accept that that was all there was to it. I still had a little doubt. But despite that, I was determined to try."

"So I started reading my Bible and did the best I could to begin obeying His statutes, laws, and commandments, because back then I had no one I could talk to about it. That is until one day, as I was praying and praising Yah, I felt as though heaven had opened over me and Yah showered down something like rain. I started to speak in tongues, and I knew from that moment on that I was truly walking in the will of the Father, because Yah had confirmed it in me when He sent His Spirit."

"You see, Yah doesn't just fill anyone with His Spirit. That is reserved for His children, and I know that I know that I am a child of Yahuah. I never blasphemed the Ruach. And you know what? Yahusha never came to you in a dream and told you He would not save you. That was Satan or one of his demons, because they can masquerade as spirits of light."

Rick was passionate as he spoke about Yah to David. He walked over to David and crouched down beside his chair and said, "Another thing, my brother, that lets me know that the Most High is not through with you is this: you slipped a moment ago and started to separate the false image from who Yahusha really is. My Ahk, how would you even know to wrestle with that unless the Spirit of Yahuah was dealing with you?" Rick smiled at David, then stood up, placed a hand on his shoulder, and said, "Yahuah the Father is calling out to you, man. He wants you."

David hung his head so that the tears in his eyes would not show. "I don't know, man."

"You know, you have one more month on this earth. I'm sorry to say it like that, but it's true. Not many people get the opportunity of knowing when they're leaving. You have an opportunity to never die. I wouldn't want to know, but you do.

Some didn't wake up this morning, and someone else did wake up but still died in a car wreck, or from a heart attack, or something else. They didn't have the opportunity you now have."

"Look, I'm not going to force you to serve Yah, because Yahuah is a gentleman, and He doesn't force anyone to accept Him. You come because you choose to answer the call. Many are called, but few are chosen." Rick then patted him on the shoulder and walked away.

The Bible study continued on for an hour more, and then the inmates left to go back to their cells.

That night, as David lay in his cell, he thought about his wasted life and how he still had never accomplished any of the goals he had set for himself, but that was neither here nor there because he would be dead in a month.

He also started to think about this salvation thing. Over the last four months he had heard about Yahuah being so merciful and loving, but he could not understand it because he had never really been loved after his mother had died. Now he heard that the Most High—the One who created everything—

loved him and always had. Incredible. David sat up on his bunk and began to talk to Yahuah.

"Yahuah, I don't really know what to say to You except that I want to be saved from this death—but I know that I have to pay it because it is a consequence of what I did to that poor girl. I don't really have an excuse except to say that I truly, with all my heart and might, am sorry, and I have so much regret that it eats at me every single day. I don't really want to go to hell. I want to have a relationship with You. I do believe that You sent Your Son Yahusha, and that He died and rose again and now sits at Your right hand. I believe it all—everything in the Bible. I just need Your help because I still find it hard to believe that You would want me. But if You will have me, then I want You."

By this time David had begun to cry, and it was frightening for him because he had not cried since he was a child. He continued to talk to Yahuah. "Most High, I am sorry for killing that girl. She did not deserve to die. I had no right. Please forgive me. I am sorry for not trusting and trying You sooner, but I did not think it was possible. I am so sorry. Please give me a chance to serve and know You better with the time I have left. I want to wake up in glory with You. I want to know You, and I want You to call me friend. Please, Most High!" David was past crying now; he was sobbing. He was pouring out his heart to Yahuah, and it felt good.

He had never in his miserable life done anything like this before. He continued speaking to Yahuah. "Most High, I am going to do this thing called stepping out in faith. I'd like to ask You for a sign to show me that You've heard me, but if it would mean more to You for me just to believe You, I'll do that. I will believe in Yahusha's name."

When he was finished talking to Yahuah, he smiled. He felt a warm, comforting presence settle on him, so he got ready to thank Yahuah for letting him feel something he had never felt before. As he opened his mouth to speak, something strange happened. He began to speak in a language he had never heard or uttered before. To him it was strange, though, because in his head he knew every word he was saying, although it came out of his mouth differently. He knew he was praising the Most High. HalleluYah! He knew that Yah had answered his prayer, because the Most High never gave His Spirit to just anyone. That was reserved specifically for His children.

David's Ministry

David was excited to tell Moreh Rick what Yahuah had done for him the night before. Moreh Rick rejoiced with him; it was a sight to see. For the next three weeks, David worked with the new inmates who would come to weekly Bible study or Shabbat assembly, just like he used to do so that he could leave his cell. He shared his testimony and led many people to Yahusha—both Israelites and Gentiles.

He had a ministry now and was able to see the seeds he had sown into other people's lives. He lived hard those last three weeks of his life and gave himself over to Yahuah to be used mightily. It was wonderful to witness the change in him.

However, Steve still came every day to taunt him, but David did not argue with him anymore. Instead, he told him about the love of Yahuah and His Son Yahusha, but Steve would laugh.

One day, a week before the execution, Steve came to taunt David yet again.

"Hey, loser—preaching your Yahusha again?"

"Hey Steve, I was hoping you'd show up. I wanted to let you know that I'm out of here in a week, but I want you to know that I hold no anger or anything against you. I know that it's your job, you know. I also want to tell you that Yahusha is loving and will forgive you, man. No matter who you are, if you just humble yourself and repent, He is faithful to forgive. I want to make peace with you before I leave." David put his hands through the bars to shake Steve's hand, but Steve snatched his hands away from the bars where he had been holding them.

"I don't need to make peace with you! You are a murderer, and let me tell you something—that Yahusha talk isn't going to work for the likes of you. You're going to die, killer. Die. Maybe justice will finally be served with your death." Steve sneered.

"Honestly, I understand your anger with me, Steve, but I have to let you know that I'm not afraid of next week, and I am not ever going to die. 'To be absent from the body is to be present with Adonai.'"

"Whatever, loser! I can't wait to throw that switch and watch your eyes close in death." Steve walked away.

David was a little hurt, but he gave it to Yahuah. He also asked Yah not to hold Steve's sin of not being able to forgive against him, because he had already forgiven him.

The End, The Beginning

The night before the execution, Steve went to bed with gleeful anticipation of the day to come. He couldn't wait to get up in the morning and head into work. He was going to flip that switch with great pleasure.

Steve brushed his teeth and washed his face in preparation for bed. As soon as he was done, he went into his bedroom and kissed his wife goodnight.

"My, you seem very happy tonight." Steve's wife snuggled a little closer to her husband.

"I am. Tomorrow I am going to do the world a great favor and send a murderer to the gates of hell where he belongs," Steve said self-righteously.

"Well, that's good, honey. Too bad there aren't more good men like you in the world." She kissed his cheek.

"That's true," Steve agreed. They both then fell asleep.

The hours passed slowly, and the couple slept soundly. At four-thirty the next morning, when the alarm went off, Steve's wife reached across him to turn it off. She then looked down at her husband and said, "I hate when you do that, hon. You're closer after all. Get up, Steve; it's time to get ready for work! Steve? Steve?"

Sometime during the night, Steve had died of a heart attack. He had awakened to what felt like bricks on his chest. The pain had been so intense that he could not bear it. He closed his eyes and felt a popping sensation. When he looked down, he could see his body still lying on the bed, and fear gripped him. Then he felt himself being pulled toward something, and instantly he was in a dark black tunnel where he could feel himself being dragged downward.

He could smell better than he had ever smelled in his life, and he could see things more clearly as well. He stopped in front of what seemed to be large iron gates, and a huge ugly creature was standing there.

Steve yelled in fear, "What is this place? Where am I? What's happening?"

"You're dead, and you're right where you belong," the hideous creature said.

“This doesn’t look like heaven! I’m a good person. You’re lying!” Steve screamed.

Something caught his eye behind the creature, and he looked closer in disbelief. His mother was standing there, crying and shaking her head.

“Oh, my son, my son, what have I done to you?” she cried.

“

What are you talking about, Mother?” Steve cried.

“You might as well come in. This is your eternal home. You’re in hell, and there is no way out. Why didn’t you seek Yahuah’s Son, Yahusha, my son?”

“No!” Steve screamed. He was shoved through the gates of hell by the hideous creature, who gave a spine-chilling laugh, and then the gates were closed.

Later that day, as David was being led out of his cell by the guards, Moreh Rick walked up behind him and draped his arms around David’s shoulders.

“I’m not going to say much. I just want to pray with you as we walk, if that’s okay with you?”

“Absolutely, Moreh.” David said.

“Abba Yahuah, we thank You for Your goodness and Your grace. We thank You for Your faithfulness, and we thank You, Yahuah, for David. We pray that if there is any malice or unforgiveness in our hearts, You would eradicate it from us now. We go in peace, and we pray that You will receive Your son David as soon as he closes his eyes to this world. We thank You, Yahuah, in the name of Your Qodesh Son, Yahusha. Amen.”

Moreh Rick then had to leave David in the waiting room by himself because they were standing outside the chamber used for the execution.

“May the Most High give you peace too, Moreh Rick, and thank you for helping me know that there was hope for me. Thank you for showing me that Yahuah still had something for me to do even here behind bars and on death row. I hope that the fruit I leave behind will remain and multiply.”

“It will, my friend. It will.”

The guards then led David away and prepared him by hanging the fluid bags and inserting the I.V.s into his arms. He was then raised up so that he could face the family of Miss Fisher. He had no family of his own there.

He was then asked whether he had any final words, and he nodded yes.

"First, I would like to thank the Most High, the Creator of heaven and earth, for this opportunity to address you all again. I want to say to the family of Miss Fisher that I am truly sorry for what I did to your precious daughter. I had no right to say what I said to you that day in the courtroom, and I hope one day you can find it in your hearts to forgive me. I would also like to apologize, although words will never do justice after everything that has already taken place. What I am trying to say is that I am so sorry that I took your daughter, sister, friend, and whatever else she may have been to others. I am so sorry for what I did to her. She did not deserve it.

I would also like to say that I am thankful to Moreh Rick for his patience and diligence in telling me about Yahusha and my relation to Him, His Father, and our people as Israelites. I am glad that he did not give up on me. I'm ready to go."

Then David turned his face away from all of the eyes staring at him. The table was lowered, and the guard was about to leave the room when a thought came to David's mind and he asked, "Where's Steve? I haven't seen him yet."

"Ah, he died in his sleep last night. Had a heart attack," the guard explained.

David was shocked but managed to compose himself a little. Finally, the time had come for him to be put to death, and the signal was given to begin the sequence of events. The first thing David felt was the cold I.V. fluid go into his arms, and instantly he could not move. Then he could feel his insides begin to shut down, and he died—but he didn't. As soon as he closed his eyes, he opened them into a brilliance beyond explanation, and there was Yahusha standing with His arms open, and next to Him was his mother, who had died when he was a little boy. They ran to him.

WOW! I am truly amazed at the love and grace Yah has given to us. Even the most hardened people can be changed. You see, Satan uses strategic maneuvers in order to keep us bound, and sometimes because of that we feel hopeless. We have unfortunately believed the lie. But through Yahusha our Mashiach we are more than overcomers. You see, there are no good people per se; we take on Yahusha's goodness when we come to Him and take on His ways. We begin by applying His Word and obeying His laws, statutes, and commandments. And rest assured, Yah is not going to let your enemy have the last laugh over you, just like He didn't let Steve have the last laugh over David. Yah is your champion. Oh, and when you die, you never really die. WOW!

Interview With the Devil

Ring! Ring!

"I'm coming! Goodness, whoever's on the other end of that phone must have no life," Dawn said sarcastically.

"Maybe if you actually sat at your desk instead of walking the halls constantly, people wouldn't seem so desperate," Charles said back to her in an equally sarcastic voice.

"Whatever." Dawn rolled her eyes and then turned her back on Charles. "Hello? Dave Fox Show, Dawn speaking, how may I help you?" Dawn sat down behind her desk and picked up a pen. "You're who? Oh, really? Okay. Well, let me take your number and I'll have him call you back. Of course I will. You have a fabulous day as well. Bye-bye."

"You were rude, Dawn. You know we are not supposed to talk to people that way. We don't bring our problems to work—or maybe just you are excluded." Charles said. He then walked over to Dawn's desk. "Are you all right?"

"Oh yes, sorry. I wasn't really trying to be rude, though, you guys. I mean, we all play around here at being rude and all, but this guy was something else."

This time Sara got up from her desk and walked over to Dawn. Sara was Dave Fox's personal assistant. They all worked for NFIC Television Broadcasting Corporation. The Dave Fox Show was one of NFIC's most profitable late-night talk shows.

"Well, what happened, dear, to upset you so?" Sara placed a comforting hand on Dawn's shoulder.

"Well, this guy just called, asking to speak to Dave," Dawn said.

"Okay, you should have transferred him right over to me, honey. I am, after all, Dave's assistant," Sara gently rebuked.

"I was going to, until he said he was the Devil. I mean HaSatan himself." Dawn looked into each of their eyes.

There was a deadly silence in the room. Then Charles threw back his head and began to roar with laughter. Dawn, seeing Charles's mirth, began to laugh as well. Others began to laugh as Charles and Dawn explained what had just happened.

"And you say the Devil left a number he could be reached at?" one of the coworkers barked out. "What's it say? Six, six, six?" More laughter followed.

Dawn reached for the number and looked at it, then laughed again. "As a matter of fact, it does. It says 666-7666. I don't even think there is a number that can be reached by that. Should we try it?"

They all began to laugh and dare one another to try and make the call.

"Give me the number!" Sara's voice cut like a sharp knife through all of their laughter. Her face was set with such seriousness that the laughter died down. Again, she extended her hand. "Give me the number, and then all of you get back to work."

"Why should we listen to you?" Charles felt offended at her tone.
"First, because the call was for Mr. Fox and I am Mr. Fox's assistant, and second, because the call was real."

"What are you saying? That Lucifer—HaSatan, the Devil himself—has called looking for Mr. Fox? Are you mad?" Dawn asked.

"I am saying precisely that. Mr. Fox will be quite pleased. He has been trying to get the Devil to come on the show for almost eight years now, and the Devil has always ignored our calls or turned us down. He said he would come at the appointed time. I have never understood what he meant, but Mr. Fox seemed to understand. I think this might be the appointed time. So, the number please."

The paper with the number was passed from Dawn to Charles, who then passed it to Sara.

"Thank you." Sara then walked over to her desk and picked up her phone. She mumbled a few words into the receiver, and before she could even hang up, Mr. Fox came out of his office and snatched the number from her outstretched hand.

"I want all of the guests for tomorrow night's show canceled, and I want the show to go live with no editing. This is going to be the most important interview of my life! You are all to be in the studio tomorrow night to watch the taping," Dave announced excitedly.

"Mr. Fox, he did not say he was coming on the show. He just said that he wanted you to call him," Charles said, scratching his head. "How can we cancel guests? We have that comedian woman who was so outraged by the war coming on tomorrow.

If we cancel her, we don't know if we will ever be able to get her back again."

"Believe me, this was prearranged. As soon as I got this call, I was told that the next day I needed to be prepared for him to make an appearance. I am prepared. So please just do as I say. Sara, please pack up and let's go to lunch. I cannot work anymore. I need to go over some things with you. I believe there are some things about me you should know."

"Certainly, Mr. Fox. My pleasure. Let me just get my coat and purse." Sara gathered her things and then left the room with Mr. Fox.

"That was weird. He has changed so much in the past month. I can't really explain it, you know. Just different. He doesn't even laugh at some of the jokes he would normally have laughed at anymore either," Charles said to everyone in the room.

"I know. We would flirt back and forth with each other," Dawn said.

Everyone looked at her with disgust.

"What, trying to get a promotion?" Jenny, one of the mailroom girls, implied rudely.

"Don't be an idiot, Jenny. All I'm saying is that we used to play like that—nothing serious, and it never would have come to anything. Lately he has been very standoffish, like a changed man."

"Well, it doesn't matter now. We need to cancel the guest for tomorrow night's show and set everything up. I think this is ridiculous, letting some psycho come on the show to parade himself before the public as the Devil. The Devil—come on, you guys." Everyone was in total agreement that it was totally wrong to let the people think the man coming on tomorrow night's show was the Devil, considering there was no such thing as a devil, but they were NFIC employees and had to do their jobs. As a matter of fact, the name of the company had only been changed to NFIC two months earlier, and no one knew why. They were just happy not to have been laid off and replaced with new staff.

Dave sat across from Sara in the dimly lit restaurant. He had been keeping this terrible secret for the last ten years, and he was glad that the secret was coming to an end. He ordered his meal from the waiter and then waited patiently for Sara to order hers as well. Then he took a deep breath and asked, "So, what are you feeling?"

"What? Oh, you startled me." Sara jumped and then laughed. "What do you mean?"

"With this whole devil thing. What are you thinking? It's important to me."

"Oh, I don't know. I know that it is important for you to have this man on the show, considering we have been trying to get him on the show for the past eight years. What I don't understand is why you call him the devil. Is he so evil that you would label him like that, or is he in a gang or what? I don't understand that, but I am glad that he is coming so that we can have some closure." Sara took a sip from her glass of tea.

"Well, yes. I understand your confusion, Sara. I am going to explain a few things about myself before I reveal my secret to you." Dave sat back and smiled to himself, then looked at Sara.

"When I was a young child, I remember being hungry and going to dumpsters to find food. I remember not having running water or electricity, and none of it seemed unnatural to me because it was all I had ever known. That is, until I went to school and saw the other children in their clean white shirts and me and my sister in our dingy white or gray ones."

He looked at her to see her reaction and, finding none, continued. "I never knew we even smelled awful until I smelled the fresh scent of the girls as they walked by. I would compare myself and my sister to them, and so I knew we were different. It went on like that throughout elementary school, but when we got into junior high and high school, we would go to the gas station and wash up at night, and we always took a shower after gym. My mom was not always home, and we never knew our father, so it was a hard life."

"Mr. Fox, you don't have to continue. This is none of my business," Sara interrupted.

"Oh, no, Sara! Don't worry. I take great joy in telling you this story. I am not ashamed." Dave smiled. "I tried different jobs after high school, but I could never get ahead, and I had a mother who was on drugs to take care of, and a sister. I did not want my life to be for nothing. I was willing to do anything—and I do mean anything—to get out of the poverty I was used to living in. I was tired of being tired. I was tired of the water getting cut off, or the electricity, you know? Having to borrow money until my next check came so I could pay people back."

The waiter interrupted Dave as he brought them their meals. "Thank you." Dave waited while Sara placed her napkin in her lap and took her first bite before continuing. "Anyhow, I remember shouting, 'Come on, give me a break!' Then, out of nowhere, a man appeared and told me he could help me."

"You mean poof—someone just appeared?" Sara asked mockingly.

"No. I mean, not long after I made that statement, a man came into my life, and from that point on my life was changed forever. I started doing comedy, and people really thought I was funny, and I was in great demand. One year later, I was offered my own late-night talk show, and I have been doing that ever since."

"Oh! I think I get it. Are you trying to say that this devil guy, whom you choose not to name, was the foot in the door for you? And now he wants you to reward him or something?" Sara was outraged that this man would try to use Dave in this way. "What I don't get is why he is doing it now. I mean, we have been trying to get the man on the show for the past eight years. Why now?"

"Because ten years ago, when he promised to make me rich and successful, he made me swear in blood that I would honor my vow and repay him when the time came for payment. I believe he is ready to be paid now," Dave said calmly.

Sara looked at Dave in wonder. How could the man be so calm when he was being blackmailed for money? "Okay, so how much money does he want? Are you actually going to pay him?" Sara asked.

Dave took a sip from his glass and then wiped the corners of his mouth. "He doesn't want money from me, Sara. He wants my soul. Ten years ago, when I made that pact in blood, I sold my soul to HaSatan for fame, and now he's come for the payment I promised."

Sara was both shocked and frightened. "You cannot be serious, Dave."

"I am, Sara, and I promise that what I am telling you is the truth. He showed me my future, and I saw it with my own eyes. I was desperate, and so I did what I thought I needed to at the time. The urge was so great I couldn't resist. So now you know." Dave looked to see what kind of effect this was having on Sara.

"I can't believe this is true." Sara was shaking.

"Well, believe it, for it is true."

"What are you going to do?"

"I guess we will have to wait until tomorrow night. I know this is a great shock, and I am not immune to your feelings, but don't worry about it, Sara. I just needed to tell someone, and I trust you. Eat your dinner. We will worry about tomorrow when it comes." Dave placed his hands on top of Sara's and gave her a reassuring squeeze.

****

"I can't believe I let you talk your father and me into coming here, Tracy!" Mrs. King said to her eighteen-year-old daughter. "It's freezing out here!" Mrs. King was thirty-six years old and her husband was two years older than she was. They had allowed their daughter to talk them into coming to the taping of *The Dave Fox Show*, even though she had not really wanted to come. Her husband had been the one to make the final decision, and now here they were.

"Mom, this is so exciting! I know that you don't care for these kinds of shows and all, but I just had a strong desire to come tonight. I got it about a week ago and bought the tickets in faith. It was like Yahuah was telling me we should be here." Arriyanna was trying hard to get her mother to understand what had compelled her to come, but she didn't think she was getting through to her at all.

"I don't know if Yah really wanted us to come or not, but we are here now, so I hope they'll let us in soon," Mrs. King said.

"Well, honey, it doesn't look like we will have to wait long. The line is moving," Mr. King said in good humor.

The King family were Israelites who had come to accept Yahshua as their Mashiach, and they loved Him with all their hearts. Mrs. King was not into attending what she called worldly events at all, so she could not pretend she liked Dave Fox very much. She had heard the jokes he usually cracked in the past about Israelites being fake and just didn't find his sense of humor humorous at all.

"Great. The sooner we go in, the sooner we can leave," she said with a smile.

"Oh Mom! Chill out and have fun for once." Arriyanna laughed.

"I am fun! You silly goose."

"I just know in my heart that Yahuah has called us to be here tonight," Arriyanna said.

"I doubt it," Mrs. King said back.

"We're next," Mr. King said, in order to cheer up the group.

****

"Has the guest arrived yet?" the frantic producer yelled.

"No! He hasn't even called, and I can't reach him at that number he gave us. It says it's not a working number. I don't get it. Dave was able to reach him by it yesterday. What the heck is going on here?" Charles was devastated. In all the years he had worked at *The Dave Fox Show*, he and the other staff had never experienced anything as disastrous as a guest not showing up. "Can we get anybody here at the last minute?" the producer wanted to know.

"No! I tried to get that comedian woman back on, but her people said she had made other arrangements. I think that is our cue to never bother asking her again, because she won't come." Charles was frantic now as well. "Where is Dave? Does he know—or even care—that we go on in two minutes and we have no guest?"

"Care about what?" Dave walked in on his way to the stage.

"You don't have a guest! The devil man never showed up."

"He'll be here. Go ahead and announce me. I'm ready." Dave readjusted his tie, and after hearing Charles announce him in his usual tone, he walked out to thunderous applause and cheers from the audience.

****

"Oh, look, Mom, Dad, there he is—yeah!" Arriyanna stood up with the rest of the audience and cheered. Mr. King stood as well, cheering and clapping.

Mrs. King stood and clapped just for the sake of appearance. The audience was truly happy to see Dave, and as they finally sat down to hear what funny opening joke he would tell, they were shocked to see how serious his face was.

"I want to welcome you all here tonight and thank you for coming. Tonight is truly going to be a historical night, because on tonight's show I have a guest coming on that I have been trying to get here for the past eight years. I am happy to say that he is finally here. So I would like to bring him out now. Lucifer, come on out." Dave turned in the direction his guest would normally walk out onto the stage from, and there was an eerie silence.

****

"What in the world is he talking about? Nobody is there! Is someone there? Am I missing something?" The producer was beside himself, as were the rest of the staff. There was no one there. Who in the world was Dave talking about?

"Charles! Terrence! I don't believe it, but look at the monitor—a man just walked out!"

"That's impossible! He would have had to come by us. How was this done? My goodness, I'm going crazy!" Bob the producer had to sit down.

"I know it is impossible, but it just happened," Charles said, staring at the monitor.

It was impossible because they were on the other side of the curtain that led to the stage, and in order to get to that stage you had to walk by where the staff was congregated and open the curtain to go out onto the stage. Yet there on the monitor was a man dressed in a white tailor-made suit. He looked like a Greek statue with jet-black shoulder-length hair and dark eyebrows. His eyes were a penetrating black, and his teeth were a dazzling white. This was all just too impossible.

****

When Dave made the announcement for Lucifer to come out onto the stage, there was an eerie silence. Everyone waited, not knowing if someone would actually come out for sure. When the man in the white suit came out, there was a collective gasp and then thunderous applause. The man in the white suit graciously accepted the applause and cheers as if it were his due. Then he took the seat Dave indicated he should take.

****

"Daddy, this is a sick joke! I am so sorry I made you and Mom come."

"Arriyanna, you and Leslie need to begin to pray, and I will pray as well. I don't think anyone understands, but I sense in my spirit that this is real. Just have faith in Yahshua and begin to pray. That is HaSatan." Mr. King began to pray that Yahuah would protect the audience.

****

The audience finally settled down, and Dave sat down as well. "I want to thank you for coming tonight. I am thrilled that you are finally here—and quite surprised as well," Dave said.

"Well, you know, I am happy to be here as well. I've had pressing issues to attend to, and I wanted to settle some business while I was in town," Lucifer casually purred.

"Oh. Well, for the sake of our audience, can you tell us a little about yourself?"

"Absolutely. What would you like to know?" Lucifer sat up with a big toothy grin.

"Well, are you really as bad as everyone says you are?" Dave asked with a smile.

"Of course not! I'm really just misunderstood. You see, everybody automatically thinks I am this terrible serpent-like creature with horns and a tail. That is not me at all. I am really a charming guy. I want to bring joy to people everywhere."

"And how do you do that?" Dave asked.

"Well..." Satan then looked at Dave with a bemused expression on his face. "Say, for instance, someone is lonely and they cry out to the Most High to help them and, of course, you know, He doesn't come through. Then I will help them. You see, you can always turn to me." The audience looked surprised at one another and then began to clap. Some of the people foolishly even began to plan how they might get the Devil to give good things to them.

Dave waited for the applause to die down before asking his next question. "So, are you saying that the things you do for people are better than what Yahuah can provide?"

HaSatan's eyes took on a sinister gleam. "Absolutely! You see, with me, as soon as you ask me, I give it to you—fame, fortune, looks, the person you want in your life, or the person you want out of your life." HaSatan began to laugh at his witty response, and the unknowing audience joined him.

"Oh, well then, if you only want to do good things for people, why would Yahuah kick you out of heaven? And how come you have no access to Paradise, where the forefathers and saints of Yah are, and which is the place we as men all hope to go? Although you and some of your minions now walk the earth, why would hell and the lake of fire be your final destination—which most of us certainly don't want to go to?" Dave asked with an innocent face.

"Because He did not. I chose to leave on my own, along with my faithful followers."

"Really? Well then, can I ask you something?" Dave asked.

The Devil looked at Dave with barely suppressed rage. "Why not? You seem to be on a roll."

"Well, according to the Bible in Isaiah, I think it is, I read that you were an angel of light and were kind of like the choir director in heaven, but you became prideful and wanted to place yourself far above the throne of Yahuah, and so He kicked you out of heaven." Dave laughed. "I also read that Yahshua said you were a liar and not only that, but that you were the father of lies." Dave laughed again at the words he had just spoken, which caused the audience to laugh as well. "Wow—to be the choir director one minute and then sentenced to hell the next must be awful! To be in Yahuah's presence one minute and then the next minute eternally separated? Wow! How can you stand it?" Dave was still in a festive, jovial mood.

Satan opened his mouth to speak but was cut off by Dave. "Boy! I read in the New Testament that when Yahshua was hung on the tree and died, He went down into the inner parts of the earth and, with a great show, snatched the keys of death and hell right out of your hands. Can you tell us what that was like?" Dave was laughing hard now.

HaSatan was visibly angry now.

****

"Daddy, why is Mr. Fox purposely provoking the Devil?"

"I don't know, but I do know that Yahuah has encamped His Malakiym here in our midst," Mr. King said confidently.

"John, how do you know?" Mrs. King asked.

"Because I can see them on the stage and all around the audience. They are standing wing to wing, like linked angels. It's awesome. HaSatan sees them too." Mr. King's eyes shone with wonder. "Abba Yah, I pray in the name of Yahshua that You would open my wife's and daughter's eyes—and the eyes of any other believer who may be in the audience—so that they may see that there are more here for us than there are of those who are against us."

Supernaturally, Yahuah began to open the eyes of His people who were there in the audience, and they could see the twelve-foot-tall Malaks with their wings touching one another. Behind Dave, one of the Malaks looked up and addressed the people of Yahuah.

"Yahuah your Elohim says to pray in the name of Yahshua for His protection now! For tonight you have been brought to this place for such a time as this, and the nonbelievers here and watching by television will see the glory of Yahuah and many will believe. But many will be as Pharaoh was in the days of old, and their hearts will be hardened."

Then the Malak once again bowed his eyes to wait on Yahuah, and the people of Yahuah began to intercede.

****

"What the heck is this circus show? Can someone tell me what in the world is going on?" Bob was yelling at anyone who would listen.

"I don't know what is going on, and I don't care. Look at the ratings, and keep that camera rolling no matter what. Do you hear me, people? No matter what!" the executive producer yelled into all of the cameramen's earpieces.

Dave was still laughing when he paused for breath. "I'm sorry. Let's begin again."

HaSatan interrupted Dave and spoke. "Enough about me. Why don't we tell the people about you?"

Dave's laughter disappeared. "Tell them what?"

"Well, how about starting out with the fact that ten years ago you were nothing but a broken-down bum struggling to get by when I came into your life and put you in the position you now hold so dear. It was I who gave you fame and power and wealth and happiness. It was I who came to you." Satan was sitting forward in his seat now, leaning toward Dave.

"And your point is what?" Dave challenged back.

"My point is this: don't you dare sit here all holier-than-thou and try to embarrass me in front of the people, because I don't embarrass easy. You needed me and I came to you, and I am here now."

"That's right—you are here now, but I have been trying to get you to come on my show for the past eight years."

"I was busy. I can't be everywhere at one time, you know?" HaSatan snapped at Dave.

"Why not? Yahuah can. He's omnipresent," Dave said.

"Shut up! I'm here now, and I want my part of the deal. I want your soul!" HaSatan shouted.

The audience gasped in dismay. At first, all this had seemed entertaining, but now it was no longer amusing.

"Well, Lucifer, I'm sorry, but I can't give you my soul," Dave said in all seriousness.

The audience and the backstage crew became terrified as, right before their eyes, the charming, handsome man they had all referred to as the Devil transformed. The lights in the studio turned gray, and the stage on which Dave and the Devil sat became a spotlight.

HaSatan became ten feet tall, and his skin took on a lizard-like texture. He suddenly grew the tail and horns he had said he never possessed, and his tongue became like a serpent's. "You dare refuse to give me the soul you vowed to me? Then I will take it by force!"

Satan slithered around the desk to tower over Dave.

****

"This is some crazy stuff, but keep rolling," the executive producer exclaimed. "Oh—and if someone knows how to pray, then pray."

****

At first the people in the audience screamed and began to run toward the exits, but they could not get through the doors because of some type of force field. Many cowered by the doors, while others remained in their seats, praying to anyone for help.

The people of Yahuah remained unafraid because Yah had opened their eyes, and not only could they see HaSatan for who he was, they could see every evil spirit in the place. They also saw the warriors of Yahuah, and as they looked at each other they could see that they were all dressed in the full armor of Yah.

****

No one in the audience, including the people of Yahuah, could understand why, throughout all of the shenanigans the Devil displayed, Dave remained unmoved. As HaSatan slithered around Dave to tower over him, Dave sat in thoughtful silence looking at his hands on his desk. He looked up at Satan and, in a calm voice, said, "HaSatan, Yahuah, the Elohim of Yashar'el, rebukes you in the name of Yahshua His Son."

HaSatan recoiled as if hot water had been thrown on him. "What did you say?" the Devil hissed.

"I said, Yahuah, the Elohim of Yashar'el, rebukes you in the name of Yahshua His Son." Then Dave sat up and looked at the audience. "He's right, you know. Ten years ago I did sell my soul to the Devil, and I became rich—very rich. I was debt-free, and I could now do things I had only dreamed of, but everything I did came with a price." Dave had tears in his eyes.

"In order for me to get the things I wanted, someone died or lost a job or got kicked out of the position I wanted. I became depressed and miserable. I had just gotten this show, and although I looked happy—a young guy with his own talk show—I wasn't. I began calling the Devil, trying to get him to come on the show so I could pay back my debt. I just wanted it over with, you know. I didn't want to continue, but I had to wait for the Devil."

Dave then wiped away his tears and smiled. "But you know what? The Devil should have come when I called, because I met an incredible woman about two and a half months ago.

She wouldn't have anything to do with me because I was self-involved. She actually called me a heathen." Dave laughed at the memory. "Anyhow, to make a long story short, I thought I was hell-bound until I found out that there was One—and only One—who could cancel my debt to HaSatan, and that One was Yahshua our Mashiach."

HaSatan became furiously angry when he heard this and began to curse.

"In the name of Yahshua, cease and desist that foul language, you devil," Dave declared. "You see, people, I gave my life to Yahshua, and He introduced me to our loving and forgiving Abba Yahuah, and He became Adonai of my life. I learned that Satan is a liar, and he deceives the world into believing different lies—like that we have time, or that there are many paths to Yahuah, or that if you sell your soul to him you are forever lost. I came to show you that it is not true. HaSatan is not all-powerful. He himself is submitted to Yah and His Son Yahshua, and Yahshua has given us power to resist the Devil!"

Dave then turned to HaSatan and said, "Devil—to you, all your foul demons, and even human spirits that are wickedly soul-traveling and are here with you now—get thee behind me now, in the name of Yahshua!"

And just like that, HaSatan and his demons disappeared.

"The Most High Yah has allowed me this opportunity to display His power and His glory. He opened my eyes to His Word in Deuteronomy chapter 28, among many other things, by letting me know that I was an Israelite, and that He had come to fetch me by opening my eyes to the truths of this world. He let me know that a great awakening was approaching and that I was a part of it. He let me know that His Son's name was Yahshua and not Jesus, and that He was the Lamb sent to restore Yashar'el and the Yahudin to the Father. HalleluYah! Some of you will be awakened tonight, but many of you will try to intellectually decipher what just took place here and will remain asleep. Don't be the latter."

Dave went on to explain the great deception, with the information available to him, and to tell the people about who the true Israelites were. He also spoke about the covenant Yahuah had made with the ancestors of the true Israelites and what Yahshua's sacrifice had really done for them as a people. However, there were both Hebrews and Gentiles in the audience, and some thought it was a Hollywood trick, while others had a seed instilled in their hearts, and Yahshua would come back for them later when Abba began the great awakening. All in all, Yahuah allowed something spectacular to take place. He allowed people to see that He was real, with no questions asked. He revealed His power!

****

The King family had been placed in the audience for such a time as this, so that Mr. King would pray a simple prayer for Yahuah to open the eyes of the people.

And Yahuah did!

WOW! Isn't Yahuah awesome? Even when some people make what might seem like the ultimate sin of selling their souls to the Devil, that sin too can be cleansed if Yahuah grants it. There is no sin too great for the blood of Yahshua to cleanse. Only the sin of blaspheming the Ruach HaQodesh cannot be forgiven—not only in this age, but in the age to come. So don't let HaSatan deceive you into thinking there is no hope. There is always hope as long as you still have breath in your body. And there is a loving Elohim who is the only source of real joy, who truly loves you and is waiting on your call. Let Yahuah show you His love today. WOW!

The Little Clay Pot

In the Beginning

"Maurah, have you seen my father?" Henry asked the young chambermaid who was obviously on her way to do an errand for the lady of the house.

"No, but I can only guess he is where he always is—in his workshop making pots."

Henry smiled at the girl as she passed and said, "I know. I should have known."

Henry's father made clay pots of all kinds for the castle. If someone wanted a good, durable pot, they would come directly to Henry's father. Of course, there were other pot makers in the land, but no one could make pots like Henry's father.

Henry left the corridor and went downstairs past the servants' quarters to a room in the far corner of the keep. Inside the room, Henry's father was busy adding water to a big, thick lump of clay in the center of the table. Henry watched as he tore medium-sized chunks from the big lump, making twenty medium-sized balls.

"So here you are again!" Henry made himself known.

His father smiled at him and said, "Yes, of course—you should have known. I need to make some new pots for the kitchen. Cook has broken two, and I know that Miss Kettles needs a new pot for gathering milk when she milks the cows. So here I am." He chuckled with good humor.

"You're incredible, Father! Why don't you just let Miss Kettles send away for the pots instead of busying yourself down here in this heat?"

"Aw, my son, it is not as hot as you think, and I have the windows there for fresh air. The fire for burning the pots is out in the yard. I have been doing this so long that I could never think of giving it up. I enjoy making these pots; it is a part of who I am. I will have these pots ready by the end of the week."

"If it makes you happy, then so be it." Henry went and found himself a stool to sit on so he could watch his father.

He could remember, as a little boy, coming to watch his father create beautiful pots. He thought it fascinating. As he grew older, he could not understand how his father made the time to make pots and do all of the other things he did as well.

Right now he watched, as he had many times before, as his father wet his hands to knead the clay. He would then take a lump and place it on a spinning wheel. As the wheel spun, he would take his wet hands and make a hole in the top of the clay, wetting his hands every so often. He would also use different types of tools to shape the mold. It was fascinating to watch a large lump become a vase or jar or jug.

Today, however, his father was not actually creating a specific container. He was making identical pots of the same size and same style. It took him a couple of hours, but the time seemed to pass quickly. When he was finished, he placed the clay pots on two shelves—ten on each shelf, five long and two across. He then turned to his son and motioned for him to follow.

They both left the room and closed the door behind them.

The Clay Pots

As the door closed behind Henry and his father, the little clay pots began to come awake.

"Aw, good morning!" the littlest pot yawned. He sat on the top shelf in row five, behind pot number five. He was pot number ten.

"Yes, good morning!"

"Hey! Who said that?" Pot Number Ten asked.

"I did. Look down here on the floor by the table you were made on."

And so all of the pots looked down to the floor next to the table on which they were made, and there they saw a chisel. It was the chisel the master used when he made them.

"Hi, Mr. Chisel!" the little clay pot said.

"Hi, Little Clay Pot. I see you guessed my name. Hello to you all. I am happy to meet you."

"What is this place?" said Pot Number Fifteen.

"This is where you come to be molded and remolded and chiseled and spun and painted and prepared to be given for a specific purpose. You are jars of clay, but one day soon you will serve a specific purpose. That is why you were made," Chisel explained.

"What specific things are we being made for?" asked Pot Number Five.

"Well, I know for a fact that two of you are going into the kitchen for Cook. She needs new jars, and I know that Miss Kettles needs a new jar to gather milk," Chisel told them all.

"Well, I hope I am not called for such a trivial job," Pot Number Two said, rolling her eyes.

Chisel smiled at Pot Number Two and said, "That is not a good attitude to have, my dear. You see, there are no trivial jobs for you jars of clay. Each of your roles is vital and important for this world as we know it to run. So never belittle another's duty in life."

"Whatever. I know that I deserve more than someone pouring milk from a cow into me or being in a hot kitchen all my life," Pot Number Two grumbled.

"I don't care what I am as long as the potter uses me," the littlest pot said—Pot Number Ten, the one behind Pot Number Five.

"Don't you worry, Little Pot. The master uses us all." Chisel smiled. Then Chisel heard a noise and said to all of the pots, "Shush. I hear the master and his son returning."

So the chisel and all of the pots closed their eyes and were quiet.

The Master and the Pots

There were footsteps on the floor outside the door. Henry and his father walked back into the room, and Henry's father went over to the shelf and pulled down pot number three, number four, and number five. "Okay, Son, I am going to take these three outside and prepare them for Cook and the milkmaid. You get the other fifteen and also bring some paints. We will paint them out in the yard so they can dry in the sun."

"Very well, Father. Do you need your chisel as well?"

"Oh yes—absolutely!"

So they gathered up the clay pots and the chisel and left. The only two pots remaining were Pot Number Nine and the littlest pot, Number Ten.

"Wow, just you and I are left. I hope we leave soon too," Pot Number Nine said to the littlest pot.

"Me too." Pot Number Ten was a little sad because he wanted to hurry out and serve his purpose.

"Oh well. I'm going to rest. You get some rest too, Little Pot."

"Okay." So the little pots went to sleep and slept so deeply that they did not hear the master return and put Chisel back on the floor by the table. They also placed a beautiful jar on the table.

Pot Number Nine and Little Pot were so tired that they slept the whole night away, and it wasn't until the next morning that they woke up.

"Good morning!" Little Pot exclaimed.

"Good morning," said Chisel and Pot Number Nine.

"Who are you?" Little Pot asked the beautiful jar on the table.

"I am Pot Number Two."

"What happened to you? You are so beautiful!" exclaimed Pot Number Nine.

"Well, unlike you, I was chosen with the other fifteen to go into the castle to decorate the dining hall, but they started to paint me this hideous color and ran out, I am glad to say. So I suppose they are here to right the wrong. I wish they would hurry. I am sick of having to stay in this hot, smelly little shop." Pot Number Two rolled her eyes.

"That is not a good attitude to have, Pot Number Two. You should be happy to have this opportunity to shine. You should not complain like you do. It is wrong," Chisel told Pot Number Two.

"Who are you to tell me what to do? You are nothing more than a chisel—a tool—and we have nothing in common, so please keep your opinion to yourself." Pot Number Two shouted. She then puckered out her lip and said, "Good, that old man is coming now so he can fix me up and put me back where I belong. Goodness! It took long enough."

Chisel looked very hurt because of the way Pot Number Two had talked to him, and Pot Number Ten was shocked that someone would talk that way at all. They both sat up straighter as the door opened and Henry and his father walked into the room.

"Okay, Father, what color did you say you needed?" Henry walked over to the paint shelf to await his father's instruction.

"I am not sure I have the color anymore, Son. Plus, this jar here has so many lumps in it, it is not worth saving. If I had not already put paint on it, I could have broken it and started over, but it has too many problems right now for me to try and deal with. I need something that is usable right now. Get a new jar off the shelf, and we will just throw this one into the trash."

So Henry took Pot Number Two and tossed her into the trash, where she shattered into small pieces. He then went to the shelf and picked up Pot Number Nine.

"You seem to have a lot of this gold paint here, Father. Shall I get this one for you?" Henry asked his father.

"No, Son, I am saving that one for something special. Just get that cream color over there and let us hurry and finish this pot here." So Henry grabbed the paint he needed, then picked up Pot Number Nine and left the room. His father followed a few minutes later.

Chisel and Pot

As soon as the door closed behind them, Little Pot yelled toward the trash, "Pot Number Two! Pot Number Two!"

"Hush, little one. Pot Number Two can no longer hear you," Chisel explained to the littlest pot.

"Why?"

"Because she is now broken. She was unusable. She had flaws that could not be fixed." Chisel tried to comfort him.

"Oh." Little Pot was even sadder. "I think I will rest now." So Pot Number Ten rested all that day. The next day came and went. Then the next week came and went. Soon time seemed to go on, and still Pot Number Ten stayed on the shelf.

"Oh Chisel, am I unusable? Master still hasn't come back to use me, and I want to be used so badly. Why has he forgotten me?" Little Pot cried.

"Little Pot, Master hasn't forgotten you. You will get your turn when it is time; it is just not your turn now," Chisel told him.

"Well, he comes in here all the time, but he never uses me. He came in here a week ago with a big new lump. He made five new clay jars. He took them out of here to the big fire stove and burned them until they shined. He and his son then painted them all beautifully like they did the first of my brothers and sisters, and yet here I still sit. It's not fair. He passed me up the first time, and now he has passed me up again. I don't think he plans to use me." Little Pot cried.

"He will use you when it is your time. Be patient and wait," Chisel encouraged.

So Little Pot waited and watched day after day as Master came in and made new pots and took new pots out and used them. Little Pot even placed himself on the table where he was made so that when Master came in he would see him, but Master just picked him up and put him back on the shelf.

Little Pot decided he could not bear to be forgotten and figured there was no purpose for him, so he knocked himself over onto his side and began to roll off the edge.

Chisel looked up and shouted to him, "Stop, Little Pot! You'll fall and break yourself!"

"I know," Little Pot said sadly, and rolled off the edge of the shelf onto the floor. He broke into seven different pieces.

"What have you done?" Chisel cried. He then straightened up with tears in his eyes because he could hear footsteps outside the door.

"Oh Father, look—that little jar has fallen and broken. I'll pick it up and throw it away for you."

"No! I was going to break it sometime this week myself. I made it a little smaller than the others. I needed to break it so that I could add more clay to it and remold it. It is a special pot to me. It was the first pot out of the lump. I have very special plans for it."

So Henry's father picked up the little clay pot and placed him on the table. He then got a little hammer and broke the pot into smaller pieces. He added water to the broken pieces and more clay. Then he picked up the mixture and started to knead and roll and squash and stretch and pull at the dough. Henry's father then rolled the clay into a ball and wet it again. He placed the clay on the spinning wheel.

As the clay began to spin, Henry's father stuck his finger into the top of the clay, causing a big hole to appear. He also used his other hand to keep it steady. Longer and longer the neck of the clay became, until it looked like a long vase. Henry's father lovingly used Chisel to etch in designs. When he was finished, he took the clay vase off the wheel and placed it on the table.

"Well, Son, I guess I will leave the clay jar here to dry overnight, and in the morning I will put it in the fire and paint it. I need to have it ready for tomorrow night."

"Indeed. You know, Father, I have never in all my life seen you use such care as you did today on that little clay pot," Henry said in wonder.

"Well, that is not true, Son. I use that kind of care with all of my vessels. It is just that I saved the best for last, and it took a little more detail." He smiled at his son. Then, after he had cleaned his hands, he draped his arm around his son's shoulder, and out of the room they went.

His Purpose

Chisel was nervous as he hopped around the table so that he could face Little Pot. He had had to climb up on Chair, who had slid closer to the table so he could see for himself. There he could see Little Pot's face clearly. He crept closer and cleared his throat. "Hum, excuse me, Little Pot, can you hear me? Little Pot? I know that you can hear me, and I know that you are still you, so please say something."

Little Pot opened one eye and then looked around. He then opened the other eye and looked around. When he saw Chisel, he gave him a small, shy smile, and then, when Chisel smiled back, Little Pot's smile became brilliant. "Chisel, it's really you! And look—it's really me!"

"Of course it's you. What did you think?" Chisel asked.

"Well, I did not expect this. Look at how tall I am. I thought when I rolled off the shelf that that would be the end of me. I even felt myself breaking before I passed out! But look at me. Why did Master fix me up? He could have used another pot. I thought I was gone forever. Remember when Pot Number Two was broken? She never came back, but I did. Why?"

"Well, you came back because you had purpose. You were made for a specific reason, and nothing else could take your place. Master made you for whatever it is he called you for. It's okay that you were broken; he would have needed to break you anyway so that he could give you what you needed to be taller.

So he had to break you, then remold you, and now you're going out to the fire. After that you will know what you were called for. Be of good cheer, Little Pot. I know that you wanted to destroy yourself like Pot Number Two."

"You see, the difference between you and Pot Number Two is that she had too much mess and so many lumps that she was unwilling to get rid of. So when she was broken, she was still unusable because she was too full of herself, and in the long run it led to her destruction. You didn't have any excess paint or mess, so Master was able to break you completely and rebuild you. Isn't it wonderful?" Chisel asked.

"Yes, it is indeed." Little Pot smiled. He then went to sleep, because he knew he had a long day ahead of him.

Early the next morning, Henry and his father returned for Little Pot. Henry went and picked up the special gold paint his father told him to get, and they left to go outside to the brick fire oven. Little Pot was placed in the fire and turned and taken out, and then he was placed in and turned again. He felt so awful in the fire; it wasn't a good place at all. He was left to rest for a little while, and then Master came and began to paint him all gold. He also took out other paints and began to decorate him, and he felt all warm inside. Little Pot was left to dry in the sun for the rest of the day.

That night a young man who was not Master came and picked him up. Little Pot was very afraid because he didn't know what was going to happen to him. He thought Master would come back and get him, but he did not.

Little Pot could see that he was being carried into the big castle again and that he was going down a long hall with doors on every side. They walked for what seemed a long time, until they came to a door at the end of the hall. On the other side of the door, Little Pot could hear many voices raised in joyful conversation.

The young man holding Little Pot opened the door and walked through. The lights were burning and the music was playing beautifully. As Little Pot was being carried into the room, people stopped to gaze at him and say wonderful things. They passed into another room, and Little Pot looked up and saw all of the other little pots who had been made with him and the ones who were made after him. They were lined up on shelves—one shelf on one side of the wall and another along the opposite wall. There were ten vases on each shelf.

Little Pot smiled because he was so happy. All of the other pots were decorated beautifully, and they smiled in wonder as they saw him. He watched them stand a little straighter as the man carrying him placed him in the center of the table. The people came into the room to look at and admire him, and he could hardly believe it. He had never expected anything like this would ever happen to him. That is why he had thrown himself off the shelf that day.

A few minutes later there was the sound of trumpets, and a man came forward to announce, "Ladies and Gentlemen, it gives me great pleasure to introduce to you His Majesty, King James Othello Rowe, and his son, Prince Henry!"

Little Pot waited anxiously, like everyone else, for the King to arrive. He had never seen a king, and he felt very fortunate that he was going to see one now.

The King made his way through the crowd, shaking the occasional hand and bowing his head to all the curtsying being given to him. He made his way straight toward Little Pot and picked him up and turned around with him in his hands to face the crowd. Then he said, "I want you all to see this treasure here. I made it myself. It means everything to me, and I have saved it for the last. You all have been able to enjoy my other creations throughout the past couple of weeks and months, but I would like to introduce you to my finest work of art. I call it My Menar."

Little Pot was shocked. All of this was for him! Master was really the King, and He had made him. He had saved him for the last because He wanted him to be the best. Little Pot was so happy. He looked around at his brothers and sisters, who smiled back proudly at him.

"I told you, Little Pot. Master uses everyone He creates—even me!" Chisel winked from the fireplace.

WOW! Isn't that awesome? We think that because God is not using us right now, He has forgotten us and placed us on a shelf somewhere in forget-me land. That is far from the truth, though, because you see, God uses all of us for different purposes. Just be patient and wait on Him. You are a little pot, and your King is saving you for last because you are His best. WOW!

The Race

The Announcement

"I pledge allegiance to the Flag of the United States of America, and to the Republic for which it stands, one Nation under G-d, indivisible, with liberty and justice for all."

The class then sat down to listen for announcements. Some of the boys threw spitballs at one another, but a stern look from Mr. Douglas settled them down.

Over the PA system, the student announcer cleared her throat and then began to speak. "Good morning! We would like to wish everyone who has a birthday today a happy birthday and a great day. The seniors' dance has been canceled and will be rescheduled at a later date. Also, Mr. Henderson would like to announce that the signup forms for anyone who is interested in the five-mile charity race can be found in the gym in his office today after school. So, anyone who wants to run can sign up then. Also, whoever enters the race will receive a prize, but those finishing in the top ten percent will get the privilege of meeting 2022's winner, Colby Todd, who won the gold medal for the twenty-mile run. And that's our announcements for today."

Then the PA was turned off and class began as usual. In Mr. Douglas's class, Darnell Evans smiled. He was going to go and sign up as soon as school was over for the day. Darnell was slightly overweight, but he didn't care. This was something he had wanted to do for a long time, and meeting Colby Todd would be the icing on the cake. So Darnell continued to smile to himself.

To Darnell, it was even more important to meet Colby because he had recently been in the news because of a scandal. He had stood up in an acceptance speech and thanked Yahuah of Yashar'el for the honor of allowing him to win his race. It caused such an uproar with the public that many of his sponsors withdrew their support, but he remained firm. Unfortunately for those who tried to destroy him, their plan backfired, and he gained even more people for the Kingdom of the Shamayim. People became curious and started doing their own research. So Colby became someone Darnell really wanted to meet.

Science Class

Troy Adams was a handsome seventeen-year-old, and he knew it. The girls loved him, and the guys looked up to him and showed him the utmost respect. Troy was athletic and an all-around, most-likely-to-succeed athlete. So when he heard the announcement, he thought this would be another great trophy to add to his collection.

Troy looked over at another student named Ron, who was just as handsome—though, as far as Troy was concerned, not as good-looking as he was. Unfortunately for Troy, the girls thought Ron was cute too.

Troy decided this would be his opportunity to show everyone that he was a better athlete than Ron. So he called out to him, "Hey Ron! Are you thinking about entering that race?"

"No, not really. I don't really want to take the time to train," Ron said over his shoulder.

"Really? Or are you just scared? Too far for baby to run?" Troy laughed. Only a few others joined in. Troy was popular, but maybe his popularity was based on fear as well as his looks.

"Naw, man. I'm not afraid. It just didn't matter to me one way or another. It's not a very big deal," Ron said with a shrug.

"Well, I'm going to enter. Why don't you enter so we can see what you've got?"

"I'll think about it the rest of the day. I don't know if I want to go through all I'll have to do in order to be prepared. When's the actual race?" Ron asked.

"I think it's in about a month, but the signup is today after school," Sara James spoke up.

"Well, I'll still think about it," Ron said.

"Your call, man!" Troy challenged.

Ron turned his head and shook it. Troy could be so arrogant, and people simply allowed him at times to do as he pleased so that they could avoid confrontation. Ron hated that Troy had singled him out because he was unimpressed with Troy. So the fact that he had challenged him to a race really didn't mean anything to him. He thought he might just enter the race so that he could condition himself. He would think about it the rest of the day.

Sign Up

"Look at that fat dude signing up!" Troy laughed at Darnell as he bent over the signup sheet. "What is your purpose, dude? Who's going to carry your fat behind when you pass out? Do you think they'll have tow trucks next to the ambulances?" Troy laughed loudly, and so did some of the others with him.

Darnell stood up and turned to face Troy. His cheeks were red with embarrassment. "I know it looks funny to someone like you to see me enter this race, Troy, but I am going to make it. So keep laughing. I don't care." Darnell ran away from the signup desk.

"You're such a jerk, Troy. When you make jokes like that, you make yourself look like a fool." Ron shouldered Troy as he made his way up to the desk. Then, looking at Troy, he began to walk away.

"Who are you calling a fool, fool? You want a piece of me?" Troy puffed out his shoulders and punched himself in the chest.

"What an idiot. That doesn't intimidate me. I'm not going to fight you. I don't need to fight someone to prove I'm a man. I'm a man because I have character, which you lack." Ron then walked off.

"I can't wait for this race to get here. I'll show that fool who's better." Troy turned to his friends, who agreed with him.

Training

The next day after school, Darnell began working out. He decided that he would start with stretches and then work himself up to running two laps.

Ron was a runner, period. When he had lived in Germany with his parents before being stationed back in the States, he ran cross-country. So getting into shape would not be too hard for him, but it still took dedication.

As Ron was running around the track, he saw Darnell out in front of him. He had to admit that Darnell looked like an unlikely candidate, but with perseverance and dedication, he could do it. Ron picked up his pace in order to catch up with him.

"Hey Darnell! I see you're really working hard at this running thing," Ron said.

Darnell had to catch his breath, but he managed to say, "Yeah, this is my first time training, so I don't know what I'm doing, but I'll eventually get it. I wouldn't have entered if it hadn't been for the fact that I get to meet Colby Todd." Darnell said this with a smile.

"Well, there's nothing to it. I'll be here every day after school, so you can train with me. How about that?" Ron asked.

"Wow! I would like that a lot!" Darnell couldn't believe that Ron Anderson had volunteered to help him with his training. Ron was so cool.

"Well, after you run this lap, go ahead and do some more stretches and then walk home. Don't do too much today. Tomorrow we'll start the hard stuff." Ron then ran off in front of Darnell.

"Okay, Ron! See you tomorrow," Darnell shouted.

Just then Darnell heard laughter and looked up into the bleachers, where Troy and his friends sat laughing at him.

"Ha! Look at that fat cow trying to run! You look so pathetic. Why don't you just give it up?" shouted Troy.

Darnell didn't say a word. He just kept running. He wished he could be like Troy and not train, but he knew in his heart that he wouldn't make it if he didn't. It took all of his might just to do those two laps.

So the training began every day after school. Ron was there to coach Darnell, and Darnell began to respond to Ron's coaching techniques. By week three, he was able to run three miles at a great pace.

Every day after school, Troy was there faithfully to tease them both. Ron encouraged Darnell to ignore Troy because he was actually doing very well. Darnell had even lost fifteen pounds. The only thing Ron regretted was that by the time of the race, he would have only gotten Darnell up to running four miles. Darnell would be on his own during the race.

****

Troy, on the other hand, rarely ran or trained that whole month.

"So, man, when are you going to start training? It's been three weeks, and all I've seen you do is some stretching and two or three laps around the track," Clarence asked. Clarence was one of Troy's closest friends.

"I don't really need to train too much. I'll probably just exercise and stuff. I won't really need to work out until a couple of days before the race," Troy bragged.

"I guess you know best—you're the runner. But why are they working so hard and you're just chilling?" Clarence wanted to know.

"Because they're losers, and losers have to work harder in order to run with the big dogs, Clay. You should know that." Troy looked at Clarence as if he had lost his mind.

Two days before the race, Troy started running around the track and found it easy to run the mile. Troy figured that if he could run the mile that well and that fast, then training was unnecessary, so he stopped and decided to just kick it. It was, after all, only a five-mile race. He would ace that easily.

Race Day

The crowd gathered around at the starting gate for the run. The starting gate had been positioned four miles away from the school campus, and the last mile would be run at the school track by running four laps. The contestants were scattered throughout the clearing in little groups, talking.

"I want you to know, Darnell, that I am very proud of you. I mean, man, you have come a long way! So be proud of yourself too," Ron said, slapping Darnell on the back.

"I am very happy, and I'm glad you took the time to help me. No one has ever done what you have done for me before."

"No problem."

That was the moment Troy decided to make himself known. He, along with Clarence, walked up to Darnell and Ron laughing.

"Hey losers, what's up?" Troy cackled. "No, really—what's up?"

"Look, Troy, I don't want any problems from you. I just want to run my race and finish. That's it," Darnell said.

"Well, you're wasting your time. This is a race filled with people who run every year, and you're out of your league, my friend." Troy snickered and walked away.

"Look, man, don't worry about it. You'll do well. We are going to run together. That way we'll keep it at a steady pace. We'll do that for the first four miles, and then after that we'll pick up the pace. At that point you'll probably be very tired, but you won't be as tired as the rest of the runners, who I believe will probably start out really fast. So keep up with me, because I kind of have a feeling for what your pace is, okay?"

"Oh man! I can't let you run slowly with me. Just go ahead and run your race, and then I'll just do the best I can," Darnell told Ron.

"Trust me. I know what I'm doing."

****

Over the excitement of the people standing near the start of the race came the sound of a man speaking through a bullhorn.

"Okay, all runners, you have exactly five minutes before the race begins! So if you still don't have a number, I suggest that you go get one now or you'll be disqualified."

Five minutes later, the runners positioned themselves behind the starting gate. Ron could see Troy pushing his way to the front. Both he and Darnell were close to the back.

"On your mark, get set, go!" the announcer yelled.

The runners took off at a fast pace—all except Ron and Darnell, that is. They didn't exactly go slow, but they did go at a pace that was comfortable. The first mile was easy, and so was the second. They passed many of the runners who had started out very fast. Some were now walking, and some were bent over holding their sides. Others had slowed to a slow jog. Still, Ron and Darnell kept their steady pace.

At the beginning of the fourth mile, they ran into Troy, who was walking with his arms raised above his head and his hands supporting it from behind. He was breathing very hard. When he saw Ron and Darnell run by, he was too tired to make a mean remark. He had to just watch them pass him by.

Sweat was dripping off Darnell's forehead into his eyes. He wanted to stop and rest so badly. He wanted to give up because he was so tired. Finally, not being able to take it any longer, he said, "I can't go on anymore, Ron. I'm tired."

Ron had mentally prepared himself for this race and had worked so hard that it was really just a nice jog for him. He knew the real race would begin at the track, but when he heard Darnell say what he did, it broke his concentration.

"No, Darnell! I'm not going to let you do this to yourself. You've come too far to turn back now. You've worked too hard, man. Keep your eyes on the prize—on the prize!" Ron looked up and said, "Look, Darnell, there's the school! All those people are waiting for us, and look, man, there are only five people in front of us! You can do this. Think of the prize and all that you've had to do to get here."

Ron hit him on the back and continued, "When we hit that track, man, I'm sprinting the rest of the way. I don't know what you're going to do—whether you sprint or jog—but I do know this: you're going to make it. Do you hear me?" Ron smiled.

Darnell smiled back. As they passed by the screaming crowd that led to the entrance to the track field, Darnell thought of all the people who had laughed at him when he signed up. He then thought of the hard training he had gone through. He thought of all the weight he had lost, and he could feel his feet moving faster. He also thought of Ron and how he had never given up on him and how he had encouraged him throughout the whole training process. His back became a little straighter, and he thought about the prize—meeting Colby Todd face-to-face, which was his lifelong dream. He took on a new determination.

Darnell thought to himself that he hadn't come this far to turn back now. Of course, as soon as they had entered the track field, Ron had shot out like a bullet and was now on his way to taking first place, and that still left the other five runners in front of Darnell.

However, as he kept moving, he passed three of those runners. He kept running, and though his legs became a little wobbly, he kept going and did something he had never done in his life: he finished a race! Not only did he finish the race, but he also placed by coming in fourth.

Ron came in first, and then there were two other runners, and then Darnell. Darnell was so happy that he couldn't think straight. As soon as he had crossed the finish line, Ron was there to hug him, help him jog down to a walk, and finally stop.

The crowd clapped and cheered for them all. It was an unbelievable day for Darnell.

It took an hour before the rest of the runners were able to assemble and the awards were given out. Troy Adams never showed up. It was said that he was so humiliated that he didn't bother to finish the race; he just went home.

I guess he should have worked out.

As for the others, they were all given ribbons for their participation, and the top four were given trophies. Ron was given the largest one, and the next size was given to second place, and so on.

Ron and Darnell, along with the other top ten runners, were all escorted to their school gym, where they received the best gift of all: they met Colby Todd.

WOW! Perseverance! We are all in a race, and we cannot expect to be successful if we only pick up our swords—which are our Bibles—every so often. We need to praise our Abba Yahuah. Our ruach needs to work out. We need to feed our hearts and souls, and we need to trust in Yahshua our Mashiach. We have to follow Abba's laws, statutes, and commandments. That's a part of the race. Don't give up. Stay the course. You've come too far to give up now. You have a cloud of witnesses in heaven cheering you on! And like Ron, Yahshua is cheering you and me on. He certainly hasn't brought you this far to let you give up on yourself. So we will see you at the finish line! WOW!

The Creatures of UHG

Once upon a time, in a far-off land, there lived a community of small, bland creatures. They were called Uhgs. Uhgs were almost round, but not really. They were mostly shapeless, but you really just couldn't tell. They were gray in color, and the only difference between the males and the females was the fact that the females had eyelashes. Otherwise, they all had big brown eyes and dots for noses. Their mouths were straight lines under their noses, and they rarely smiled. When they did, you really couldn't tell, because their mouths would then resemble a crooked horizontal line.

Some Uhgs were tall and some were short. Some were fat and others were thin. On the whole, there was nothing really special about the Uhgs. The Uhgs lived their lives much like you and me. They went to work, they married and had children, and some of them attended Assembly. They were different in their worship, though. They worshiped the self-proclaimed King Hobart, which the people knew to mean "bright or shining intellect."

Hobart lived on the top of the highest hill. Hobart really wasn't anyone special. You see, one day, maybe ten years ago, he got hit by a bus and lived to tell about it. So he proclaimed that he himself was a god because he had been hit by the bus and then lived to tell about it.

Unfortunately, the Uhgs agreed and had been worshiping him ever since. Others just lived their lives, and that was that.

A Religious Family

"Bobby B! Bobby B!" Mother Sniddle yelled.

"Aw gosh! What, Mother?" Bobby B yelled back. He was slightly irritated because he had been outside playing with his friends.

"Go and find your sister, love. It's time to go worship the great Hobart." Mother said with a smile. She then turned to walk back into the house but was stopped by a question.

"Find which one?" Bobby B asked. He had two, after all.

"Twiddle, silly. The only one we have to look for every time it's time to worship the great Hobart." Mother shook her head as she walked back inside the house humming.

"Oh!" Bobby B said. He agreed with his mother, though. Every single time it was time to worship the great Hobart, Twiddle had to be found. He knew exactly where she was. She would be in the Bluebonnet pasture, looking into the sky. Twiddle was always asking stupid questions like, "Where did we come from?" "Who made the world?" and "What happens after we die?" It was especially irritating when she would ask things like, "Why in the world do we worship Hobart the terrible?" Bobby B loved Hobart. Sometimes when he went up the highest hill to Hobart's huge, beautiful house, Hobart would stand on his balcony and throw down gumdrops.

As he neared the Bluebonnet field, he saw his sister. He didn't feel like going all the way into the middle of the field, so he called from the edge, "Twiddle! Mother wants you. It's time to go and worship Hobart!" Bobby yelled.

"Go away!" Twiddle yelled. It was so frustrating to her because week after week she had to go through this ridiculous ritual of worshiping Hobart. He was nothing more than another Uhg like them all. "I'm not going, and neither should you, Bobby B!"

"Well, you better come on now or Mother will be here to get you like last time and embarrass you in front of all the others!" Bobby B reminded her.

Reluctantly, Twiddle rose up and followed Bobby B home.

****

"Oh, Twiddle, there you are! You're always the one to make us late. You really should learn to manage your time, my dear," Mother said. She motioned for Twiddle and Bobby B to come and walk with her.

Mother and all of the other Uhgs who worshiped Hobart were on their way to the highest hill, where they met weekly to dance in a circle and throw flowers. They also sang songs of praise to him. Hobart would come out onto his balcony to enjoy the songs of praise being sung to him.

"Mother, I manage my time just fine. I just don't get why we bother to do this. Hobart is an Uhg just like you, her, or him," Twiddle said, pointing first to her mother and then to two other Uhgs.

Her mother motioned for her to lower her voice because she might be overheard. "Look, we have gone over this before. Hobart is special. He was hit by a bus, Twiddle, and he lived to tell about it. A bus! Do you hear me?" Mother told her with passion.

Twiddle looked at her mother but had to suppress a smile. However, she continued because the subject was too important to ignore. "Mother, so what if Hobart was hit by a bus and lived to tell about it? My appendix ruptured inside me, and I lived to tell about it as well. I'm not telling Uhgs to worship me, and I don't want to be worshiped!" Twiddle then lowered her voice and draped her arms around her mother's shoulder. "Mother, haven't you ever looked up into the sky and thought how magnificent it is? Haven't you ever wondered how we all came to be? Look at the trees and the flowers. I mean, they are all so beautiful, and Hobart had nothing to do with it. Mom, I am sure there is more to this world than we know."

"No! I have never heard any such thing. Now be quiet. We are almost there. I expect you to worship in our circle, of course. Here are your flowers," Mother said, handing her some flowers that were to be used for tossing into the air as they skipped around in a circle.

"I'm sorry, Mother, but I am not participating this time. As a matter of fact, I am not participating in this ritual ever again. I think it is silly that you all do, but I am not going to do it ever again. I'll go sit in the grass under that tree over there." Twiddle pointed to a huge tree.

"We will talk about this when we get home, young lady. Do you hear me?" Mother said.

Twiddle went and sat down under the huge tree. She just felt it was silly to worship Hobart when he did nothing spectacular. Twiddle felt that there just had to be more to this life than what she could see. She watched as her mother and the others who had come to worship Hobart got into groups, forming circles. They would all skip and leap while running behind one another in a circle. They would toss rose petals and chant a silly song: "Oh, great and wonderful Hobart, who watches over us both night and day, may your mouth always smile at us, we pray."

Twiddle thought it was a stupid song. The passion they displayed was wasted, and she felt they should all be pursuing the truth—whatever that was.

The creatures of Uhg had been worshiping for about a half hour when a moving truck passed by. It could be seen driving toward the residential neighborhood many of them lived in. No one could see who was driving the moving truck because it was some distance away, but they could see a bright light in the driver's side of the truck.

"That was odd," Twiddle said to herself.

Worship service broke up quickly after that, which left Hobart in a foul mood—but who could blame the Uhgs? No one had moved into their small community in over twenty years. "I bet they are moving in across the street from our house, Mother. That old house has been vacant for two years. How exciting! I have never met anyone new before," Twiddle said.

"Yes, it is exciting. I'll make some pie as soon as we get home, and then later we can take it to them so that we can introduce ourselves." Mother was already picking out the recipe she would use in her head.

"Mother, did you happen to see the bright lights coming out of the truck?" Bobby B asked.

"Yes, I did, but I thought that perhaps they were reading something, you know," Mother said lamely.

"It's daylight. All they have to do is open their eyes," Twiddle said.

"Oh well, that's not important. Let us just get home. Hurry!" Mother said, picking up her pace.

****

There was a vacant house across the street from the Sniddles' house because the prior owners had moved away to a new home in town. The Sniddles walked up to their home and, sure enough, the moving van that had driven by during the worship of Hobart was parked out front of the vacant house. Others who had been with them also stopped to see who had moved in across the street. Mother Sniddle and the others observed as lights moved back and forth in the undraped windows.

Uhgs began to comment in the crowd about the lights in the windows. After what seemed like eons, someone finally emerged from the house. It was unlike any other Uhg they had ever seen. It was the same as them, but not the same, because although this Uhg—or thing—looked like them, it had the most brilliant light coming from within it.

"What the heck is that?" Mother Sniddle asked in stunned disbelief.

"Mother!" Twiddle said in shock because of her mother's language. "Why don't we just go and ask?" Twiddle made as if to walk toward the new neighbor's house, but her brother stayed her hand.

"No, Twiddle! You don't know what that thing will do to you. Oh no! Look, there are more of them! I'm going inside," Bobby B said, and he did indeed run inside.

Others in the crowd began to run as well. Twiddle, on the other hand, shook her head and began to walk across the street to find out who or what the new Uhgs were.

"Twiddle, you come back here instantly! Twiddle, you better do as I say or else!" Mother Sniddle yelled.

"Oh, Mother!" Twiddle said, but she did turn around and obey her mother because it was the right thing to do. She did, however, stop there because no matter what, she was not going to worship Hobart.

****

Twiddle and her mother, along with about a dozen other Uhgs, looked on as a smiling creature who appeared to be an "Uhg of Light" came out of the front door, followed by a smiling female "Uhg of Light," who was also followed by two smaller smiling "Uhgs of Light." They all smiled and waved at the small crowd gathered across the street from their home.

When they didn't get even one response, they simply went to the moving van and removed the last of their boxes and furniture. When what appeared to be the father of the family took the last lamp off the truck, he turned around and smiled and waved goodbye to everyone who was still standing outside.

Soon afterward, the crowd dispersed and went back to their homes. When the Sniddles got inside their home, Mother told both Bobby B and Twiddle to go upstairs to clean their rooms and bathe while she prepared the evening meal. The children did as their mother told them. When they were done, they ran downstairs as was usual and found Father Sniddle already at the table, so they kissed him and then took their places.

"Twiddle, what is this I hear about you going over to introduce yourself to the strange Uhgs moving in across the street?" Father asked.

"Oh, Father, please! I don't understand how you and Mother could be so narrow-minded. I mean, they are new, for crying out loud. I just want to make them feel welcome," Twiddle tried to explain.

"Well, I don't want you nowhere around them. I have seen Uhgs like them before. They teach a different religion than the one we practice, so I don't want them to have a chance to influence you into converting to their religion."

"Why would they do that? What is it exactly that they believe, Father? And how come you don't believe?" Twiddle asked.

"I don't believe because I know the truth. Hobart is our focus of worship!" Father said. "I don't want to talk about it anymore. I want you to stay away from those light creatures!"

"Pity." Twiddle shook her head. "Mother, Father, I know you mean well, but I cannot and will not do as you ask because you two are wrong—and if others come to the same conclusion as you two, then pity on them too. How would you feel if you were new and every time you tried to meet someone or smile, the only response you received was to be alienated by everyone? I'm sorry, but I cannot be a party to your cruelty." Twiddle then stood and walked away to her room without eating.

"Twiddle!" Mother called out.

"Let her go. She just needs time to think this over, I'm sure. Why would she want to get involved with these Uhgs anyway? Look at them—they are filled with light!" Father asked in disgust. Bobby B sat with the side of his face resting in his right hand as he looked out the window and, without even thinking, said, "Yes, but we look so drab."

"What did you say?" Father yelled.

"Nothing, sir." Bobby B stammered.

"Well, you said something, boy! Now speak up."

"Nothing, Father. I was talking to myself." Bobby B then got up from his seat at the table and went upstairs as well. He had touched none of his food. Bobby B and Twiddle sat in her room looking out the window across the street at their new neighbors' house.

Usually, their older sister Tinker was home, but Mother had forgotten that she had allowed her to stay the night at a friend's house, and she would not return until tomorrow night.

****

They had stayed up late the night before talking about the day and the new neighbors of light, trying to figure out what it all meant. Bobby B and Twiddle both agreed that they would be nice to the little Uhgs across the street because they knew that they themselves would never want to be treated that way if they were new somewhere. Bobby B was not too interested in their religion because he still loved Hobart—after all, he was all he had ever known—but right now he was more interested in making a new friend. Twiddle, on the other hand, was a little skeptical about religion in general, but she too wanted new friends, and she wanted to know why they looked as though they were on fire.

Bobby B had come into his sister's room that morning, and they once again jumped into a conversation about the new neighbors across the street.

Suddenly Twiddle saw the young Uhgs walk outside their home. "Okay, there they are, Bobby B. You stay here in case they try to do something to me. That way you can call Mother and she'll be able to help. I am going outside to talk to them now."

"Be careful."

Twiddle ran down the stairs and went outside. She stood for a few minutes and then mustered up all the courage she could find and walked across the street to meet them. "Hi! I'm Twiddle. Who are you?" Twiddle smiled, but felt so ridiculous. What a silly thing to say when you meet someone for the first time.

The two young Uhgs on the other side stopped and smiled. "Hi, Twiddle. I'm Constance, and this is my brother, Dre."

Constance walked forward and shook the hand of a reluctant Twiddle.

"I saw you all moving in yesterday. As a matter of fact, the whole neighborhood did. We first saw you when you drove by while we were up at the big mountain worshiping Hobart," Twiddle said with a smile.

"Oh, you worship Hobart?" Dre asked.

"Yes—I mean no, I mean…" Twiddle blushed red. "No, I don't worship Hobart, but my family does. I don't believe Hobart is any different than anyone else."

"Oh." Constance laughed. "Well, I guess you are wondering where we come from and what my parents do and such."

"Well, actually, no. What I was really wondering is why you are so full of light. That is odd to us. We have never seen anyone like you," Twiddle said matter-of-factly.

"Oh, well, that is because of who lives inside me," Constance said.

“Okay, so who do you think lives inside of you?” Twiddle said, trying not to laugh.

“It’s not who I think. It’s who I know. I mean, after all, I am an Uhg just like you, but I have a light in me that is very evident to all who look at me. I didn’t do it by myself, so it had to be someone, and it is the One I serve.” Constance said this with love glowing in her eyes.

“Who is it that you serve, and where is He or she?” Twiddle asked, feeling a little frustrated. All she wanted was a clear answer. She was tired of playing musical words and wanted Constance to get to the point.

“Well, Twiddle, we serve the Most High, who lives in heaven but comes down to live in our hearts when we accept what was done for us by His Son on Calvary.” Constance then told her brother to go inside to get the Word. “You see, Twiddle, we believe in one Elohim, and His name is Yahuah. We were separated from Him because our ancestors broke covenant with Him, but because of what His Son has done by sacrificing His life for us, we are now able to be with Him again. We believe that we are sinners, and sinners are Uhgs who transgress Yahuah’s laws. Those things keep us separated from the Abba, and Abba means Father.”

Just then Twiddle heard her name being called from across the street. Mother stood at the door with a furious frown on her face. Twiddle blushed and was about to turn and run off when Dre ran back outside. He was carrying something called the Word in his hand. Constance took it from him and gave it to Twiddle.

"I know you have to go, so take this and give it back later when you can. It was nice meeting you. Maybe we can be friends, and when school starts again after the summer, maybe we can hang out."

"I'd like that," Twiddle said. She then turned and ran home. Mother closed the door sharply behind her as she came inside the house, marched to the bottom of the stairs, and yelled up for Twiddle to come back down.

"Yes, Mother," Twiddle said a little nervously.

"Don't 'yes, Mother' me! You purposely disobeyed your father and me. You will stay in your room for a week by yourself. Tinker just called, and the Appleby's have asked her to go with them on a camping holiday. I gave my permission, so you'll be in your room by yourself. Do I make myself clear this time?

That means you stay out of that room, Bobby B!" Mother yelled.

"How will I eat, Mother?" Twiddle asked.

"Don't be smart. You'll come down and eat with the family, of course. Now get upstairs, and no TV. Read a book!" Mother then marched off.

Twiddle watched from the top of the stairs as her mother marched off. "I am upstairs," she muttered. Oh well, that would give her time to read this book. So Twiddle sat down and began at the beginning of the book. It said, "In the beginning, Elohim made the heavens and the earth." Twiddle's heart began pumping very fast. She was so enthralled by the story that she kept reading and reading. Twiddle had just begun to read about the radiance on the face of an Uhg named Moses when she heard her mother coming up the stairs. She hurriedly put the Word down and got out a novel when the door to her room opened.

"Okay then, you can now come on down. I know that this must be hard for you and all, being up in your room, but I will have obedience in my house! Do you hear me, Twiddle?"

"Yes, Mother," Twiddle answered.

"Good. Now go and wash up and then go downstairs." Twiddle complied, and after she had finished all of her toiletries, she ran downstairs and sat at the table. Mother prayed and asked Hobart to bless their food, although Twiddle knew he could not, and Bobby B was also coming to the same conclusion that he probably could not. The family sat down and began to eat. Every so often Twiddle would look up to see her mother or father staring at her in a most peculiar way, and she wondered why. She did not have to wonder for long because her tactless brother broke the silence.

"So, what's up with your face and hands, Twiddle? Are ya sick?" Bobby B asked.

"I don't know what you mean. I feel fine," Twiddle said.

"Well, you don't look yourself, Twiddle. Your color looks a little lighter. You look a little pale. Are you sure you're all right?" Mother asked in concern.

"Believe me, if I were sick, you would all be the first to know it," Twiddle answered, trying to reassure them. They all knew she didn't handle sickness very well, so why would they ask such a silly question? After dinner, Twiddle helped Mother with the dishes, but as soon as she was done, Mother sent her back up to her room. She was quite fine with going because she knew the Word was waiting for her. So off to her room she went. She jumped on the bed, pulled the book from under her pillow, lay down, and began to read. With every chapter, she felt something begin to tingle inside her until finally she drifted off to sleep.

****

The next morning Twiddle got up a little early and began reading where she had left off the previous night. She accidentally dropped the Word, and as she picked it up, it opened to a section that said *The New Testament*, and her heart just really began to pound. She marked her place in the chapter she was previously in and began to read the New Testament. She had been reading for a half hour when her mother called for her to come down to breakfast.

Twiddle got up and ran to the bathroom. She washed her face and brushed her teeth, all the while thinking about what she was reading. She closed her eyes and thought about the way this book said the world was made. She had also begun reading the New Testament, which explained the chronological birth order of a man named Yahshua. The book said He was the Savior to the true Uhgs of Yashar'el. She was just so excited.

Everything she had read somehow testified to her that it was true. She couldn't understand it. But all along she knew that there had to be more to this world than she could see. She knew for a fact that Hobart hadn't done all the things this Elohim Yahuah had done, and she couldn't wait to start reading again after breakfast.

"Good morning, family," Twiddle said happily.

"Good morning, my dear," Mother said from the kitchen. She was making a plate for Twiddle. As soon as she was done, she turned to walk toward the table—but she dropped everything in her hands and ran to Twiddle. "What is wrong with you? I told you not to go over to those people's house the other day, and now look at you! You are definitely changing somehow, Twiddle. Come on, Bobby B, go get in the car. We are taking your sister to the doctor." Mrs. Sniddle was frantic.

"Mother, I am not going anywhere. I have never felt better in all my sixteen years on this earth," Twiddle said.

"Well then what is wrong with you?" Mother yelled.

"Mother! Really! What is wrong with you?"

"Look at yourself! I mean, Twiddle, go look at yourself!" Twiddle got up from the dining room table and went to stare at herself in the bathroom mirror. She was shocked at what she saw. In her heart was a little flame, and it was burning softly. The soft glow of the light in her heart gave an iridescent glow to her skin. That must be why her family thought she looked sick the night before, Twiddle said to herself. Wow! That Word must be true, because not only was she changing in her mind, but her outer appearance was changing as well.

Twiddle ran out of the bathroom and ran to her mother and kissed her. "Mother, I am not sick. Please rest assured that I will be fine."

"What did that girl say to you the other day, Twiddle? I want to know right now," Mother said.

"Well, she told me what she believed, Mother, and everything she said to me made very good sense. She told me that she worshiped Yahuah and that He created the earth and the sky. She said that even we, the Uhgs, were created by Him. Mom, there is so much. Maybe by the end of the week I can sit down and tell you!"

"You go to your room right now, young lady, and when your father gets home today, he'll have a good talk with you, do you hear me?" Mother was very angry.

Twiddle was more than happy to go to her room. She did not dare tell her mother about the Word for fear that she would take it from her. She went upstairs to her room and locked the door this time because she knew her mother could come up at any time. She picked up the Word and read the first five books of it by the time it was almost time for Father to get home. She set the Word under her pillow, got down on her hands and knees, and began to pray to the Elohim she had just heard about.

"Dear Mr. Yahuah, it is so nice to meet You. I am Twiddle. All my life I have felt that there was more to this life than what we really knew about, and one day when I was older I had planned to pursue it, but it seems like You came to me first. I want You to know that I have believed everything You said in this book here, and I am thankful for the love You showed us by sending Your Son. I also would like to invite You and Him into my heart forever. I repent for transgressing Your law, but I have to find out what it is and then I will do it, so please be patient with me as I learn what those laws are because I really don't know or understand."

As soon as she said that, a brilliant light came forth from her, and she stood and began praising Yahuah. She ran to the mirror in her room and rejoiced at her transformation. Then she became fearful because her parents and everyone else would know. But she remembered also that if she were ashamed of this new relationship she was having with Yahshua, then He would be ashamed of her when He introduced her to His Father. So she wasn't willing to go through that. She knew that Yahuah was real because, come on, look at the change in her. This must be why the Uhgs across the street glowed—because they knew Yahuah—and that is why her family and everyone else in town were gray, because none of them knew Yahuah or His Son Yahshua. They only knew Hobart the imposter.

****

Outside, Twiddle heard a car door slam and somebody run into the house. She knew it could not be Father because he had come home a half hour earlier. She was curious, but she knew she couldn't go downstairs until Mother called. Suddenly there was a loud scream and voices raised in anger. Fear gripped Twiddle like a glove, and she bolted out of her room. As she came down the stairs, she could hear her mother yelling at someone, and that someone turned out to be her older sister, Tinker.

Twiddle tiptoed to the entrance of the kitchen and gasped audibly, but still no one acknowledged her presence. Sitting in the kitchen at the table was her own sister Tinker, glowing just like her. Twiddle rushed into the room.

Mother Sniddle looked up as Twiddle ran into the room. She let out a heart-wrenching scream and fainted dead away.

"Oh Mother! I hate to see how you react when I finish telling you everything," Tinker said as she went to assist Twiddle in picking her mother up from the floor. "Well, Twiddle, I see that you too have found the truth?" Tinker winked.

"I have indeed," Twiddle said.

"What have you girls done? You've destroyed our family! This is a Hobart-believing family," Father shouted.

Tinker, who was Father's favorite, went and put her arms around her dad and said, "Father, I am still the same Uhg, and I love you all the same. I did not go through this transformation for nothing. It was Yahuah the Father and Yahshua His Son who did this to me. I don't need you to believe me. I have a book I want you to read that will explain everything."

"You mean this book called the Word?" Bobby B said, coming in looking a little less gray.

"I see you've been reading it as well," Tinker said.

"I'm losing my children," Father said, sitting down next to his slumped wife, who was nursing a headache.

"No, Father, you are not. We are the same—we just now see so much more. Daddy, you and Mother and I have been wrong about Hobart. He is just an Uhg like the rest of us. We were on our way out of town when the Appleby's wanted to stop by and worship Hobart. When we got there, there were others there as well. Some were glowing and some were not. You could tell that the ones who were not glowing had dragged the ones who were glowing there in the first place. Uhgs were crying everywhere. Finally, after a half hour, Hobart came out onto his balcony—and Father, he was glowing. He came down to us himself and introduced some new Uhg who had just moved in. Apparently this Uhg was an Uhgbrew, and he said that Yahuah had called him to this part of the world to witness and to bring many to His Son. It's working. But Mother and Father, the choice is yours!"

****

It has been four months since Twiddle's eyes were opened to the truth of who she was and who the true Creator was, and her walk is growing daily. Many Uhgs have given their lives to Yahuah, have repented, and are now following His laws, statutes, and commandments, but many do not want anything to do with this new way of worship. Even Hobart comes to assemble with the new group that has been started in their land. Uhgs still try to worship him, but Hobart will have none of that. He is quick to tell them that he is not the Way, and then he witnesses. They either come to the Son or they don't. It is their choice. At the Sniddles' house, Father and Mother have begun to read the Word to find out exactly what their children are involved in. They seem to look a little less gray every day.

WOW! That Word really begins to wash you once you pick it up. If you didn't already notice, the Uhgs are really representing the spirit man inside our bodies before we accept Yahshua, who introduces us to Abba Yah. We are gray and dead-like, but once we meet Yahuah, a fire begins to rage inside our hearts. So the Uhgs are you and me before Yahshua, but once we are reborn, that Uhg turns into a glowing light that is made manifest through the lives we lead afterward. Are you gray? Or is there a fire burning in you? WOW!

Pardoned

Monday Afternoon

"Move back, dude, or they'll see you!" Timothy said under his breath.

"I'm not stupid! I see them too. You just do what you're supposed to do," Erik said back.

The boys were hiding behind a thicket of trees, watching two women pushing their babies in strollers. The women were getting closer and closer. Erik ran out from behind the trees and yelled at the women. Startled, they looked up and screamed. Timothy ran up, pushed one down, and snatched her diaper bag. Finding nothing, he rummaged around in the stroller until he found her purse and took her wallet. Erik did the same with the other woman. She, on the other hand, fought back, so he slammed her in the temple with his fist. He stood looking down at her for a moment. Fear crossed his face, and then he looked at her once again and ran off.

The boys could hear the women screaming behind them, so they ran as fast as they could. They knew it was only a matter of time before the police showed up. As they ran, they went through both purses and took out what valuables they could find. When they were satisfied, they threw the purses down.

"Hey man, let's go to my house, and then when it's clear, we can go find the gang," Timothy said.

"Okay, let's go," Erik agreed. They both made their way back to Timothy's house. Once they were inside, they ran upstairs and into Timothy's room.

"Eighty-nine dollars, dude! That was sweet!" Timothy laughed as he jumped onto his bed. "I bet that witch didn't know what hit her. You cold-clocked her, dude!" Timothy kept laughing.

"Whatever, man. I didn't want to hit her. I wish she would have just let us take the darn money. It's not like she doesn't have more. You saw how they were dressed in their fancy clothes and nice strollers. I can't stand that. Why'd she have to fight, man? Why?"

"Um? You're not serious, right, dude? Because if you are, then maybe this is a sharing thing you might want to do with someone else, because I'm not the emotional, touchy-feely kind, brother." Timothy mimicked what he thought would be a psychiatrist's attitude.

"Whatever." Erik laughed back.

The boys were just two of eleven who hung out together doing petty crimes. It seemed as if they were all invincible because they never got caught. Sure, the police had been sniffing around, but they would never suspect any of them because they were all middle-class people. Timothy had lived in the neighborhood all of his life, and his parents were well-to-do. If he ever got into trouble, Mommy and Daddy always bailed him right out. He was their baby boy.

Erik, on the other hand, came from the projects, but his father had worked very hard and finally moved them out and into this middle-class neighborhood, thinking that it would be a better way to bring up his children in a good environment. Little did he know that it didn't matter what neighborhood you brought your children up in to determine their outcome. It was more the Word and the character you instilled in them. The gang usually hung out at night, but Erik and Timothy lived close to one another, so they were together both night and day.

"Hey man, it's a long time till tonight, and we have all this money. Let's order some pizza and play some video games," Timothy suggested.

"That's what I'm talking about." Erik nodded with a grin on his face.

Monday Night

"Who's got a cigarette?" James asked.

"I guess the store does! If you can't afford them, man, then maybe you shouldn't smoke. I'm not trying to support you and me." Andrae was more of the comedian of the group.

"Yeah, okay. Can I hold one?" James asked again. Andrae shook his head and handed him one.

The group was hanging out behind an apartment complex in the ditch, trying to figure out what to do. "I know what we can do if you guys want to do something fun," Katina—one of the two girls allowed to hang out in the group—spoke up.

"What?" everyone said in unison.

"Well, remember that stuff we used to make and then fling at cars as they drove by?"

"What stuff?" Erik asked because he didn't know what she was talking about.

"Well, we used to get a big bucket and pour in flour, milk, eggs, tomato sauce, peas, and anything else we could think of. Then we would go to a street that had heavy traffic, and as the cars rode by, we would throw it on them. Sometimes the people would chase us, and it was fun."

"And it's fun, really?" Erik asked.

"Yup," Katina said.

"Then let's do this," Erik shouted.

So the kids went to their homes and grabbed the things they needed and met back up again. They mixed the concoction together. The messier it was, the better. They did argue, though, about where to do this, because none of the kids wanted to take a chance on doing it in their own neighborhood, where they might be recognized. So they walked twenty minutes down the main street until they came to another subdivision. There they found the main thoroughfare where traffic was busy. Then they began their assault.

The first car they hit honked its horn but kept going. The next car stopped and backed up, but they all ran to hiding places. The third car chased them for a whole half hour. They were having so much fun. The next car they hit was speeding, and Jarred was able to stand out in the middle of the street and hit the driver's-side windshield. The driver lost control of the car and hit the curb at a high rate of speed, causing it to flip onto its side and roll.

Erik and the other kids had not expected that. They threw down their food concoction and took off running home. Once they made it back to their own subdivision, they could hear in the distance the sound of police and ambulance sirens. No one said a word. They just ran home.

Tuesday Evening

Everyone met over at Katina's house because her mother and father's attitude was more like they would rather have their daughter and her friends at home where they could see them than out causing trouble—and that included boys as well.

"Has anyone heard anything about what happened last night?" Scott asked. He was another boy associated with the group of eleven.

"No, I was going to look at the news and see," said Sharnice. She was the other girl who always hung out with the group.

"Well, it's five, so turn on the TV."

****

"So, tell me, Mr. Franks, do you know why Police Chief Zechiah has called this news conference today?" Betty Williams from News Channel Four inquired.

"No, Mrs. Williams, but he should be here any minute." He was interrupted by the arrival of the police chief and his entourage of associates. The chief stood behind the hastily assembled podium, shuffled some papers around, coughed, and then thanked everyone for coming.

"Please be seated and save your questions until I have finished giving the information that needs to be given. Thank you. Now let me start by saying that I know you have been reporting on the accident that happened last night in the 7200 block of Timber Creek. The victim is in critical condition as we speak but is expected to make a full recovery. That victim is also none other than Charles Ray Midland, who has been wanted in the state of Washington for the brutal robbery and slaying of pizza-delivery man Raymond Moss."

The police chief paused for effect and then continued. "Mr. Midland was traveling at a high rate of speed when he was struck in the windshield with food products by unknown assailants. Because of the high speed at which he was traveling, when the car was struck with the food products, it caused him to lose control of the wheel and the car flipped repeatedly. The assailants were seen running from the scene of the crime. Although we were able to capture Mr. Midland and take him off the street, what the assailants did still constitutes a crime."

The police chief looked straight into the camera and made this declaration. "If you are or know the assailants, please have them contact the San Antonio Police Department as soon as possible. We have spoken to our lawyers and have decided that since a hardened criminal was taken off the street, we are willing to work with you and give you a full pardon—with the recommendation that you participate in a program for six months to help troubled youths."

After a brief pause, he continued. "Now, we have sources helping us, and we are pretty confident that we will have all of the assailants in custody by Friday afternoon. So, once again, we are giving the assailants the opportunity to do the right thing, because despite their crime, we were kind of helped out in a way. But they still committed a crime, and Mr. Midland was not the only victim. We received many phone calls about youths throwing food at cars that night and were actually already on the way to the scene when Mr. Midland was hit, so a crime has been committed. However, if those involved will come forward and receive the pardon being offered, then they can be placed in this program because we want to help. On the other hand, if they do not come forward, we are still confident in capturing them, and at that time we will prosecute them to the fullest extent of the law as adults."

The police chief then turned to walk away.

"I thought you were going to stay and answer questions, Chief Zechiah?" Mrs. Williams yelled out.

"I think I've said all that needs to be said."

"Well, is there a deadline or something?"

"As a matter of fact, there is. They have till Friday at noon." Chief Zechiah then disappeared back into the police station with all of the people who had come outside with him.

****

"Yeah, right!" Timothy yelled.

"Keep your voice down, dummy. My mom's right in the kitchen, thank you," Katina whispered.

"Okay, so if we turn ourselves in, then we can get this pardon thing?" Erik asked.

"Don't do this to me, man—don't do this. I'm not turning myself in, and you better not turn me in either! You can't be that stupid and think that is all there is to it. Turn yourself in and walk? Come on, Erik!" Timothy said angrily.

"Look, I'm not turning anyone in. If I decide to turn myself in, it will be me and only me. All I know is that someone almost died because of us. Timothy and I mugged two ladies the other day, and I hit one hard. I hate myself for that. I mean, they were walking their babies! I don't want my life to be like this. Heck, I could have stayed in the hood if I wanted to be a thug." Erik stood and began to walk to the door.

Timothy got up and met him before he got to the door. "Man, if you walk out that door, know that you're done with us. I mean it too, man. You'll have to watch your back."

"Please. I grew up in the projects! You think you can threaten me with your wannabe thug mentality? Please. I'm out of here!" Erik walked out.

"Anybody else who wants to leave can go too," Katina said.

Everybody sat still, and then Sharon, Scott, and Dee got up and walked out.

"Whatever. They were just a bunch of scared losers anyway," Katina said as she watched them leave.

Wednesday

On Wednesday afternoon, Katina made a phone call to Sharon.

"Hello?" Sharon said into the phone.

"Hey girl, it's me, Katina."

"What's up?" Sharon asked.

"I'm calling about the other night. I wanted to know if you guys had made your final decision. Are you all really going to turn yourselves in? And if so, are you turning us in too?"

"Look, we've talked about this before. I told you yes—we're going to turn ourselves in, in the morning. I suggest you come."

"I don't think so. I like my freedom." Katina rolled her eyes. "Look, just leave our names out of it, please."

"Fine!" Sharon said.

"Fine!" Katina snapped back.

The girls hung up on each other, and that was the last time they ever spoke. None of the other teens tried to contact one another either.

Thursday Morning

Thursday morning, all of the teens who had decided to turn themselves in met at the police station downtown. Their parents had been very angry with all of them when they found out what they had done and had insisted on going along with them.

Erik seemed to have gotten it the worst from his parents. His father had been especially disappointed considering all that he had accomplished and done in order to get his family out of the projects.

The teens each turned themselves in and were booked and processed into the juvenile judicial system. All felt betrayed as they waited in the holding tank to talk to the judge. They were held in separate cells.

About half an hour later, they were all escorted, unshackled, to stand before the judge. The judge looked up from his notes and addressed the teens. "I would first like to know if there is anyone else who should be here who isn't."

The teens didn't bother to look up.

"That's all right. I expected that. Now, I do want to thank you and your parents for showing up here today. You see, you four are here and seven are still missing. You looked surprised to see that we know there were eleven of you. Well, that is because we have witnesses who counted how many of you were standing out in the road that night. Unfortunately for you, there was someone who recognized all of you."

"Now you four will receive a full pardon, although you will do some community work and enter into the rehabilitation program we have set up just for you. It is the state's belief that if we intervene right now and approach the problem at the beginning, we can eliminate future acts of crime."

He looked up and smiled at the teens. "I have here in my possession eleven arrest warrants. There was one for each of you. Now there are only seven for the others who did not bother to come in. I'm handing each of you the one with your name on it for you to tear up. After that, you will be released to go home with your parents, who have been given all the information needed to start you in the rehabilitation program. You have all been given a second chance, and not many people get one, so use it wisely. That's all."

The teens were then released to their parents.

Friday Night

Friday morning came and went, and still Timothy and the rest of the teens who had held out continued to hold out.

Timothy had been furious that Erik and the others had been stupid enough to turn themselves in and had rallied the others around to his way of thinking. They planned to jump the others wherever they found them and hurt them badly.

They had decided to go to Katina's house and hang out there since her parents would be out for the night. The kids settled themselves into the family room. They had turned on a movie and were still discussing the plans of assaulting Erik and the others when the power was cut. There was total panic in the room because fifteen seconds after the electricity was cut, the door was kicked open and people in dark clothing with lights on their helmets came storming in.

"Get on the ground! Get on the ground!" the SWAT officer shouted.

The lights came back on, and the teens were found with their faces on the ground. A detective walked in carrying a piece of paper. He began to read off each of their names on the warrant. When he was finished, he said, "You are all under arrest for the attempted murder of Charles Ray Midland and for assaulting three other motorists." The officer then read them their Miranda rights and put them all inside one of the police vans waiting for them outside.

As they were driving off, Katina's parents arrived home, so one of the officers explained what had happened.

****

The police van exited the expressway and waited at the light on the access road. When the light turned green, it began to move forward. They never saw it coming. A drunk driver traveling at a high rate of speed ran the red light and crashed straight into the side of the van. The force of the crash caused the van to roll several times.

The driver of the car and the teens in the back of the van died that night, but the two police officers driving the van survived.

WOW! We expect every story to leave us with fluffy, happy feelings of joy, but sometimes we have to have a major shock given to us in order to slap us out of the fantasy we might be living in. You see, Yahuah is great and He loves us, but He is also just. He has given us a pardon through His Son, Yahusha. Those who receive it will be fully pardoned, and those who don't will receive sure judgment. Are you pardoned? If not, get it. It's free! WOW!

Micaiah and the Icky Bugs

The Fire

"Hurry, Son!" yelled Tyrene. Tyrene was a tall man with light-brown eyes and dark, woolly hair. He was an easygoing man—someone you just felt completely comfortable approaching. Right now, however, he was anxious. He had been on the phone and learned that a fire had broken out on a piece of property not far from a part of his land where he allowed his cattle to graze. So he needed to leave right away so he could get the cattle back across the river to a safer place before the fire overtook them. "Son, get a move on now, ya hear?" Tyrene called from the kitchen.

Tyrene's fifteen-year-old son, Micaiah, ran from his room and down the hall to the kitchen, where his father waited. He looked exactly like his father, just in a younger version. Not far behind him were his two best friends, Rusty and Dusty, his German Shepherds. "Ready, Dad. Just had to change my shoes."

They both ran outside, jumped into their black Ford pickup truck, and headed down the country road that led from their ranch to the main highway. It was about a twenty-mile ride to the site they needed to reach in order to gather the herd back across the river to where they would be safe.

They made it to the cutoff that led to the river within sixteen minutes. Tyrene had sped the entire way. "Son, that fire there is about three or four hours off. We'll have plenty of time to get the animals across the water. We'll bring them five miles onto this side of the property where they'll be safe. That fire will die out as soon as it reaches the water, but dang, I sure do hate to see all this green grass burn up."

"I know, Dad, but give it some time and it'll grow back next spring, I bet."

It took them about two hours to get all the animals across the river. They placed them in a field five miles out of the way, where the animals could graze in peace. Tyrene suggested they go back and take one last look to make sure they hadn't forgotten anything. They could see the fire off in the distance and knew it was only about an hour before it reached them.

"Well, it looks clear, Son. Let's head on home."

They turned and headed back to the pickup truck parked across the river in a gravel clearing. Along the way, Dusty and

Rusty began to bark and wag their tails wildly. No matter how many times Micaiah called to them, they stayed in place and barked all the more. Micaiah went to see what all the fuss was about. They were still about fifty yards from the river, so they really didn't have much time to waste. He had to look down over a steep ledge in order to see what the dogs were barking at. He really couldn't tell what he was seeing, so he squinted to focus better. All he could make out was that something—or rather, several things—were moving down below.

"Hey, Dad! I'm going down there. I don't know what those things are, but I can't leave them behind. I'm gonna go see if I can get them to follow me."

The Icky Bugs

"What a beautiful day! I could lie here forever," sighed Davy. He was the littlest of the group. He and his Icky Bug friends were sunbathing on a rock. When they looked up from where they were lying, they could see the clear blue sky and lots and lots of green trees.

The Icky Bugs lived in their own little paradise, where they kept to themselves and stayed away from all of the other bugs. They thought themselves too good to make friends with the other bugs and snails that lived close by. What they failed to realize was that they smelled so awful, none of the other bugs wanted to be around them anyway.

"Well, suit yourself. I am definitely going to get out of this heat and find some shade before all of this magnificent beauty of mine fades away," Lovely whined. Lovely, the only girl allowed in the little group, went to find shade.

"Hey, I have a better idea. Why don't we all go gather twigs and bring them back here to build a tent? That way Lovely can rest in the shade while we swim in the pond," Toby suggested. All of the Icky Bugs readily agreed.

"Okay, let's split up and meet back here in ten minutes. I'll take Davy with me since he's so little." Davy was offended. It seemed like every time they wanted to do something he could never do it alone because he was too little, but not today. Things were going to change.

"No! I'm not going with you. I am going by myself. How will you ever know if I can do anything if you never give me a chance to prove I can?"

The other Icky Bugs stopped to think about what he said and then agreed to give Davy this one chance, but if he failed, it would be back to being paired up with another Icky Bug at all times. So each Icky Bug went its own separate way. Davy went up toward the high mountain, where he knew there would be a lot of twigs and branches ripe for the picking—and he was right. There was no one else there. Davy was so happy. He was positive he would have the most twigs when he returned to the rock, so he started gathering them as fast as he could.

Micaiah and Davy

Davy was humming and picking up twigs when suddenly a large shadow fell over him. When Davy looked up, the most terrible sight he had ever seen was swooping down on him. He did not realize what it was, so he dropped all of his twigs and began to run. As luck would have it, he did not get too far. Micaiah saw Davy begin to run, so with his hands he swooped down quickly and picked him up. "Don't be afraid, little bug. I'm not gonna hurt you. I'm here to help you. My name is Micaiah. What's yours?"

Davy was shaking so hard he could hardly think, but he could hear the kindness in Micaiah's voice, so he answered back, "Davy."

"Well, Davy, I am not here to harm you. You see, there is a fire burning not far from here, and everything in sight is going to burn up. I saw you and all of your little friends from up on the cliff and came down here to rescue you. My dad is still up there waiting for me. I told him I had to come down here to talk to you."

"Why should I believe you? I don't smell any smoke," Davy said, sniffing the air.

"Why would I lie? And why would my father let me come down here and risk my life by climbing down such a steep cliff if it were not true?" Davy thought for a moment and realized Micaiah had made a good point, so he asked Micaiah to wait while he went to find the others.

Micaiah let Davy know that he needed to hurry because there was not a lot of time left. "While you are getting your friends together, I will hurry home to find something to bring back to carry you all home in. I just don't have anything with me. I'll also need to prepare a place for you all to live so you can be in an environment close to this one. I won't be long. Just go and tell the others and get them to hurry back here so I can save you all."

"Well, how long will that be, Micaiah?"

"I'm not sure. Just be ready. I promise to be back in time." Micaiah and Davy parted ways, one going up the cliff, the other going to find his friends.

Micaiah

"Dad! We need to hurry and get back to the house so I can get a big box or something to carry the bugs I found home in," Micaiah said breathlessly as he reached the top of the cliff. His father bent down and helped pull him the rest of the way up.

"Whew, Son, you smell terrible. What happened down there?" Micaiah told his dad about how he had met Davy and how he had warned him to go and tell the other bugs about the danger that was on the way. He also told his dad that Davy was an Icky Bug and that they just smelled really bad for some reason, but that didn't matter to him because he still wanted to save them and take them home to live with him. Micaiah told his dad that if he didn't save them now, then no one would.

Tyrene hugged his son and let him know how pleased he was with him. He was so impressed with his willingness to risk his own life in order to save others. Tyrene also let Micaiah know that he had nothing to fear because he would be right there holding a rope to make sure he pulled Micaiah back up to safety when he had all the Icky Bugs safe in the box. Micaiah hugged his dad once again, and they, along with the dogs, jumped in the truck and raced home to get the supplies they needed for the work ahead.

Davy

Davy rushed back to the place where he and the others were to meet. He called everyone to gather around him.

"Hey! What's this all about, Davy? And where are your twigs? I knew we should have kept an eye on him."

"No, wait, listen! I was up by the Big Mountain when suddenly a big shadow came over me. I was scooped up into the hand of this big human. The human told me there was a fire headed this way. I didn't believe him at first, but I do believe him now."

"Oh brother! Davy, we don't want to hear this silly story of yours. Now where were you?" Jude asked. He was one of the older boys in the group.

"I'm telling you the truth. We have to hurry and tell the others, or we will all burn up."

"Yeah, why should we believe this Micaiah guy anyway? Maybe he just saw my unbelievable beauty from afar and decided he just had to be near me, to absorb my beauty!" Lovely cried. Everyone looked at her and shook their heads. "Well, it could have happened," she snapped.

"You know what? I do believe you, Davy, and I am going to believe this Micaiah friend of yours too. If you think about it, why would this Micaiah guy come down here to let us know if it were not true? He doesn't know us and doesn't owe us a thing. There is no point. I will help you spread the word, Davy. How long do we have, by the way?"

"Micaiah didn't say. He just said to meet him back by the Big Mountain. He promised he would be right back. He said he had to go home to make a place for us to live."

A lot of the Icky Bugs believed and went to tell as many other Icky Bugs as they could, but some thought Davy had a wild imagination. Those who believed met Davy at the spot where Micaiah said to meet him. Some came only to laugh at the ones who actually showed up to wait for Davy's imaginary friend. When all was said and done, every Icky Bug in the town had been warned and given the choice to either believe Davy or not. The majority did not. Thankfully, his mother, father, brother, and sisters did.

The Icky Bugs had been waiting for nearly thirty minutes when a few started to become impatient. The ones who did not believe at all told them that they had told them so. The ones who did not believe, and the ones who grew restless, decided to leave and suggested to Davy, his family, and all the other bugs that they too should leave and go home to their comfortable houses and stop wasting their time waiting for something to show up that wasn't.

Davy and the rest of the Icky Bugs who decided to stay ignored the jokes. They looked up to the sky and waited patiently. The other bugs who had decided to leave had only been gone five minutes when a large shadow fell upon the group. Micaiah appeared with a big smile on his face. In his hand was a big white box with holes on the sides. Davy and the Icky Bugs began to jump and cheer. Some began to cry and hug one another.

Davy ran to Micaiah, crying, "I knew you would come! I knew it! I did all that you said, and a lot of the others helped too, but some of them did not believe me. That is why there are only a few of us here."

"That's okay. Let's wait a few minutes and see if they return." Tyrene yelled down and told Micaiah he was sorry, but they could not wait any longer because the fire was almost upon them. Micaiah quickly gathered the Icky Bugs into the box and started back up the cliff. The smoke was beginning to grow thick.

Tyrene kept a steady hand on the rope. As soon as Micaiah reached the top, his father grabbed his arms and helped hoist his son over the ledge. Micaiah hugged his father hard. They didn't say anything to each other, though, because there wasn't time. The smoke had become thick. Micaiah and his dad ran as fast as they could, with Micaiah clutching the Icky Bugs safely in his arms. Through the thicket they could feel the fire fast approaching them. They were almost to the river when Micaiah tripped, but his father was right there to help catch him, and he regained his balance right away. They made it across the river to the other side, and there they stopped to catch their breath. They could see the fire raging on the other side, but that was where it stopped because of the water in the river. They were all safe.

Micaiah opened the box so he could look inside to see how the Icky Bugs were doing. They were shaking with fear and crying because they knew a lot of their loved ones had just lost their lives that day because of their failure to believe. They were relieved, though, that they were still alive. Micaiah gave them a reassuring smile, then he hopped in the truck with his dad and they headed home.

Back at home, Micaiah let the Icky Bugs out into a large section of his backyard that had plenty of plant life and flowers. He had added a large bird pool that usually sat on a column into the middle of the flowers so that the bugs would have water. Micaiah had added anything else he could think of to the space in order to make them feel more at home. "I know that you all are feeling sad right now, and I am truly sorry for your loss, but I promise to take care of you for as long as you'll let me," Micaiah told the Icky Bugs.

"Micaiah, this is my family and friends," Davy said as he introduced everyone who had been rescued. Micaiah kissed and wiped away every tear and welcomed them all to their new home. They thought that their new home was much better than the old one. They settled down to begin their new life.

In the morning, Micaiah brought them out some breakfast, but when he saw them he stared in surprise. The Icky Bugs were gone. In their place, scattered throughout the garden, were white cocoons. Micaiah called his dad.

"Well, Son, I guess all the excitement caused them to go through a change. We'll just have to wait and see what happens."

New Beginnings

It was two weeks before the Icky Bugs emerged from their rest. One by one, they slowly woke up from their long sleep. They had been transformed. No longer were they ugly or smelly. They were now bright and beautiful; with colors they could not explain. They stared at one another and slowly began talking.

"Wow! You're beautiful, Lovely!" Davy exclaimed.

"What? Are you just now figuring that out?" Lovely said playfully. "I know—and so are you."

"I can fly! I can fly!" screeched one of the others.

"Hey, what do you say we fly off and explore the world?" suggested Davy's brother.

"Not me. I am staying right here. When we were ugly and stinky, not only did Micaiah risk his life to come and save us, but his father allowed and helped him. I love him. I'm staying with Micaiah. I'm here for life."

"You know what, Davy? You're right. I'm staying here too. Sorry for even mentioning it. Now let's go and find Micaiah." The beautiful bugs left to go find Micaiah, to tell him that they were his for as long as he would have them—which was forever.

WOW! Isn't that how strong God's love is for us? When we were as filthy rags—dirty and smelly with sin—He looked beyond that and allowed His only Son to save us from hell's sure fire. Now in His sight, we are beautiful. WOW!

About the Author

Sharman Castillo, known as Sharman C., is a Truth Music artist, author, and creative entrepreneur whose life, loyalty, and true love begin and end with the Father Yahuah and His Son Yahushua. Through her music and ministry, she is committed to sharing truth, stirring remembrance, and encouraging others to walk set apart in faith and obedience. Her songs and creative expressions are rooted in a desire to uplift, teach, and minister to hearts seeking a deeper relationship with the Most High.

She is the founder of SoFresh Records and SoQodesh Publishing, and also creates through SharmsbySharman Set Apart Fringes and WowStories, an audiobook series on YouTube. Whether through music, writing, or other creative works, Sharman's mission is to point others back to truth and to use every gift she has been given in service to the Kingdom. A wife, mother, grandmother, and servant at heart, she devotes her life and work to ministry, remembrance, and walking qodesh before Yahuah.

www.ingramcontent.com/pod-product-compliance
Lightning Source LLC
LaVergne TN
LVHW040220110826
845146LV00005B/1351

9798996218349